I0692744

Chrysanthe

A soft rumble and a deep exhale woke me up from my slumber.

I smiled as I turned over on the mattress, opening my eyes slowly to sunlight streaming through the window.

I turned my head slightly; that was when I saw Caliya looking at me with piercing, amber eyes.

"Hey there, sweetie," I said, grinning as I extended my arm out, scratching behind her ear; she moaned happily, shutting her eyes in contentment. "Hi."

She just continued to lean into my hand, shifting her bodyweight into mine, even though I was still in bed. I laughed; my voice was still thick with sleep.

"Aww, Caliya. I'm okay, girl."

The tiger opened her eyes back up to look at me. She blinked, a deep rumble echoing through my bones as she watched me eagerly.

"I guess it's time to get up, isn't it?"

I looked around the treehouse that I was in; sunlight drenched the inside of it, confirming the fact that I needed to get out of bed.

"Alright; time to get up," I said, stretching for a moment before throwing the sheets on the mattress back, making my way off it.

Caliya watched me silently as my feet hit the wood floor, before she yawned. Her canines were razor sharp as she extended her legs out in front of her, stretching.

But I just smiled; I wasn't scared of her at all, even though she was a tiger.

I had taken care of her ever since she was a cub, after her mother had been killed; she'd been given to me so that I could raise her to adulthood.

Given to me by an Oracle, who, when I was younger, had trained me to become the Protector of the Earth.

The same Oracle who had yet to return from her journey. She hadn't come back from bringing Altheda, a fellow Celestial Being, to her Realm.

The Realm of the Flowers, it was called.

The Oracle though, named Sybella, she hadn't made her presence known.

For several mornings, and nights.

It wasn't like her to just disappear, especially for long periods of nightfall.

I tried my hardest not to worry, for the shapeshifting Being that was once my mentor would be back.

The sound of a soft moan brought me back to myself, and I glanced down, only to see Caliya rubbing her head into my stomach.

I smiled at her as our eyes connected, and I brought my flower-tattooed hand to Caliya's ear, stroking it.

She closed her amber-colored eyes before opening them back up, a relaxed expression radiating throughout her entire body.

Caliya automatically calmed down, and I laughed at how she looked.

The tiger appeared to be completely tension free.

"Aww, sweetheart," I said, gazing into her face, "you're alright. You're alright."

ETHEREAL AFTERWORLD

Book 2 *in* The Ethereal Chronicles

ELIZABETH WITTEKIND

ISBN: 979-8-9852145-9-8 (paperback)
ISBN: 979-8-9883995-0-6 (hardcover)
ISBN: 979-8-9883995-1-3 (ebook)

Book cover design and interior formatting by Miblart.com

I brought my attention to the rest of my treehouse.

"Now, I just need to clean up before I go outside," I said, looking at my unmade bed. "I am going to fix you."

I quickly got to work, making the bed and tidying the room.

I found my hairbrush afterward, bringing it up to my scalp and then getting the tangles out of my blond hair.

When I was done, I quickly changed clothes; a completely blue dress which matched my tinted mane.

My hair had been dyed by Altheda, who had said it would help defeat Thana.

It had, but now I had a permanent hue to my mane.

I stretched once I was done. The sunlight warmed me as I smiled, welcoming the sensation.

"Okay," I said as I petted Caliya, who was right beside me. "Time to go outside."

I sighed as I came out of the forest, making my way into the clearing.

My Fate Tattoos on my left wrist, as well as my bare feet, glittered in the sun, and I could feel my face getting warm from the illumination.

I just knew by the feel on my face that my peacock feather tattoos near my eyes were brightening.

It made me feel incredibly relaxed, like I was who I was destined to be.

To be the Protector of the Earth.

To take command of the weather, and control and heal nature. I could also mend wildlife injuries and regenerate plants.

I absolutely loved my talent, as well as my Fate Tattoos.

Everything regarding the imprints was amazing, as well as the obligations they represented.

I was the Protector of the Earth, and I absolutely loved my power.

Barefoot as always so my abilities would work, I walked over the bright green grass that was incredibly healthy.

It was all so amazing, how the landscape appeared.

I had helped it become that way by defeating the Queen of Death, and by using my fated abilities.

The Queen of Death, Thana, who also had been my twin sister.

Thana, or Calla, which had been her birth name.

She'd tried to destroy the Earth, releasing Hell onto it.

I had been the one to stop her, trapping her in the Abyss, but unfortunately, I still had an ache in my gut from the fact that I had gone up against my *own sister.*

It made me feel terrible, but also relieved, since the threat was gone.

Now, though, I had to save my parents, who had been tormented by Thana.

That, and I had to figure out how to get rid of the scar that had become intermingled with the tattoo on my right arm. The tattoo of my World.

The scar was bothersome, and I needed to figure out how to get rid of it.

To save my parents, as well as myself.

I would have to speak with Sybella so that I would know what to do.

A breeze blew through my blond hair, bringing me back to myself.

I blinked, shaking my head slightly, before I petted Caliya's striped body that was right beside me.

She was staring ahead of her, watching the landscape that surrounded us.

Her tail swatted the air, and I realized she was watching a creature. A creature that was flying toward us.

I gasped as it approached.

It was a barn owl. But not just any barn owl; it was the shapeshifting Being known as Sybella.

She had returned.

2

The barn owl screeched as it got closer to me, before it threw its body forward, landing on a tree branch.

I took a deep breath, and then spoke.

"Sybella? Sybella, is that you?"

The owl looked directly at me, clacking its beak almost knowingly, and that was when I knew, in fact, that it was my former mentor.

She looked at my face, before she abruptly left the branch; Sybella flew toward me.

A white light engulfed her.

Within a split moment, Sybella had transformed into her Being self.

Vines and multicolored flower patterns cascaded down both her arms, while there was a peacock feather tattoo on the back of each of her hands.

Both intricate Fate Tattoos were illuminated in the bright sun, appearing almost hypnotic; Sybella looked at me as her imprints danced.

Her light blue eyes studied my face, her blond hair hung long; and she was wearing a turquoise blue dress.

She watched me for several moments before speaking. "Hello, Chrysanthe," she said.

I smiled, nodding at her. "Hello, Sybella," I said back. "Did you have a great trip? Did Altheda make it back alright?"

"Yes. Yes, she did, Chrysanthe."

Sybella, the Oracle, seemed to fidget a little; her eyes drifted away from me, and that was when I knew something was wrong.

My eyebrows automatically creased in worry.

"Sybella, what's wrong?"

The Oracle sighed, before looking into my face again.

"Chrysanthe, the Ethereal City is under attack."

I stood in front of the Oracle in shock, not fully taking in what she had just told me.

I blinked several times, trying to comprehend her statement.

Finally, I spoke. "What?" I asked, incredibly confused. "What?" I repeated.

The Oracle just looked at me. "The Ethereal City is under attack. Somehow, when Thana had the Empyrean Blade, a Being from Hell got loose. He flew up to the Ethereal City, where he has been terrorizing everyone ever since. He also released the Minotaur your sister had. The beast she trapped in the Abyss escaped. Both the Being and the creature have been terrorizing the City ever since."

My heart skipped a beat painfully.

My twin sister had a Minotaur?

"How do you know this?"

My former mentor just stared into my face. "I was told by Celio," Sybella stated.

I blinked, my mind whirling from all this information.

I stood in front of Sybella, confusion and surprise engulfing me.

There was so much I wanted to ask; I just didn't know where to start.

Celio. The Minotaur. The Being from Hell. The Ethereal City. The fact that the Being had released the Minotaur.

All the things that Sybella had said were just whirling around in my skull. I was unable to pick a topic for several moments.

I cleared my throat finally, and opened my mouth to speak.

"Wh…what?" I asked. "What?"

The Oracle stared at me; her blue eyes were steady on mine.

"How… how is Celio?" I asked.

Celio. My love who had gone back up to the Heavens, where he lived as the Guardian of the Spirits.

"Is Celio okay?" I asked again.

"Yes. Right now, he is. He is still in the Afterworld, but the other Archangels, as well as him, have been watching the destruction and terror plaguing the Ethereal City."

I nodded in understanding.

My breathing slowed. But then another thought occurred to me.

"The Being from the Abyss," I started, "he released a Minotaur? That my sister had?"

I shook my head in bewilderment.

Not only was Thana the Queen of the Underworld, she was the Queen of Death. Not only did she have control of the Cloaked Spirits, also known as the Wraiths… She also had control of the Banshees, the Ghosts, the Goblins, and… and… a Minotaur.

A Minotaur.

A Minotaur.

My twin sister had had a bull-like creature while she was in Hell. Sybella could see how taken aback I was.

"Chrysanthe," she said, "the Being is causing harm to the City, and is letting Thana's creature destroy everything in its path. Since you defeated Thana before, you are the only one that can go up against the Being from the Abyss."

I tried to regulate my breathing as she continued.

"You have been scarred, but there is a special incantation that I have learned long ago, one that can help you be protected in the World Beyond. Chrysanthe, you will have to go there to get help, so you can defeat the Minotaur, as well as this other Being."

"What is the other Being's name?" I asked.

Sybella looked me straight in the face before she answered.

"Acanthus. The Being's name is Acanthus."

3

"Acanthus?" I repeated, unfamiliar with the name. "Acanthus?" I said again.

"Yes," Sybella said, nodding. "He is wreaking havoc on the City; he needs to be stopped."

"And I'm the only one who can defeat him, and Thana's Minotaur?"

The Oracle looked into my eyes.

"Yes. You won't be alone, though. Celio will be there to help you too, among some other Beings, and the Archangels. They will support you, but only *you* will be able to *defeat* the threat."

My insides squirmed at the mere thought.

Even though I had ended the threat to the Realms, which had been my *own sister*, I still had to deal with a Being and a creature that she had, partly, unleashed into the Ethereal City.

Even though she was gone, I had to deal with everything she had left behind.

It made me upset and anxious.

Thana always had to make everything worse.

I sighed, looking at the Oracle again, before I spoke.

My thoughts had drifted to what she'd said a few moments ago. About the incantation that could save me, even though I'd been scarred.

Scarred by the Empyrean Blade, when I'd gone up against Thana.

"So, there is an incantation that can help me? I know I need to save my parents as well, since they were poisoned and blinded, but you said I would need to go to Heaven to find a cure. The incantation, can it help me?" I asked.

The Oracle nodded.

"That is correct, Chrysanthe. The spell will protect you from the Everlasting Light of the Afterworld. If you were to go there without the incantation, you would burn up, since you have been touched and scarred by the Empyrean Blade and your sister. You would burn up, as well as your parents, since they were harmed as well."

My parents, Viro and Thera, now couldn't be in the Afterworld. Not without my help.

I had to save and protect them again.

I guess that answered the question as to if Celio would need help saving them.

I'd told Celio before he had gone back to Heaven that I would ask the Oracle if I could help.

Sybella spoke again, breaking me out of my thoughts.

"The incantation, it can only work for a few mornings and nights; it is not long-lasting. You will have to come back to Earth so I can repeat the spell."

I nodded, trying to comprehend everything.

"How long does the spell last?" I asked, curious.

"It only lasts for about fourteen mornings and nights. After that, you will have to return to Earth, before your scar starts to hurt. Your scar hurting means that the incantation is wearing off, and that you are going to soon succumb to your injury. You would burn up in the Everlasting Light."

I gulped, and Sybella saw my face, my scared expression.

"If you feel anything from your scar, go to Earth immediately, stay out of the World Beyond, and I will be able to cast the spell again."

The Oracle just watched my eyes with her blue ones, checking to make sure that I was soaking up all the information I could.

I was, but it all made me terrified, everything that I was learning.

The Minotaur. The Being known as Acanthus. The scar that could cause me to burn up in the Everlasting Light. My parents.

It was just *a lot* to take in.

And only I was going to be able to do this. Defeat the threat.

I would have help, but this all would be up to *me.*

I stood on the grass in my bare feet for several moments, gathering everything up as the sunlight illuminated my surroundings.

My former mentor stared at me, and then spoke once more.

"Chrysanthe, you will also need the Empyrean Blade; you will need it once you get to the Afterworld."

The all-powerful Blade that had scarred me when I defeated my twin.

"I need that as well?" I asked, feeling dumbfounded.

Sybella nodded, and then moved her hands to her chest.

Sure enough, there was a tattoo above her heart; one that was the Empyrean Blade.

She grazed her fingers along her skin, and then pulled the Blade out from her flesh by the handle.

It shone magnificently, a white light flashing on the Blade edge; the Oracle gave it to me.

I took it gingerly, before glancing up at her.

Sybella's eyes met mine, and she nodded encouragingly.

Go on, she seemed to say, even though she hadn't said a word.

I took a deep breath, steadying my shaking hands before I positioned the Empyrean Blade over my heart, glancing down at my own chest.

The enchanted weapon soaked into my flesh, and I felt a powerful sensation as I did so.

It's the Blade. It's making me feel this way, I thought.

It was that powerful.

I closed my eyes for a moment, and opened them back up to see Sybella looking at me.

Her stare was steady as she saw the change in my demeanor.

The Empyrean Blade's power and strength was intense.

My back straightened up as I saw the Oracle's stare, and she took a few steps toward me, holding out her arm so her tattooed hand grasped mine.

Exactly where the scar was, intermingled with the tattoo of my World.

She placed her hands gingerly on my skin, and closed her eyes.

She said the incantation, murmuring words of a different tongue. I knew those words would protect me while I was in Heaven.

Afterward, Sybella opened her eyes, peering into mine.

"Now, Chrysanthe, you are all set to go to the Heavens. You will *have* to leave by nightfall; as I said, the spell won't last forever, so you have to get going tonight. You can say goodbye to Caliya for now, but you must go to the World Beyond by sundown. I will get Maximus for you, but you *must* be in the Afterworld when the stars come out."

I nodded my head automatically.

"Alright," I said.

"The Winged Horse will help you get to the Afterworld," Sybella repeated. "He will help you on your journey."

I gulped.

It seemed like this was going to be a bigger task than when I defeated Thana.

Bigger, and more dangerous.

But I was willing to take the chance.

To save the Ethereal City. To save my parents.

I was willing to take the journey to the Afterworld.

I looked at the Oracle. "Alright," I said, taking up the challenge. "What else must I do?"

"The Winged Horse will be here soon," Sybella repeated, before she continued. "He'll help you get to the World Beyond, where you'll meet up with Celio." Her tone had become instructive as she went on. "Celio will help you, along with some other Archangels. You'll also meet a sprite, a water fairy from the Heavenly Falls, at some point. She oversees all the creatures there, and will help you on your quest. There are many other Beings you will meet, and other things you will have to do, but going up to the Heavens and seeing Celio is the first part of this."

The Oracle stopped talking then, watching me.

I nodded, absorbing her words.

"Get on Maximus, go to Heaven, and find Celio," I said, staring at my former mentor to make sure I had everything right.

She nodded.

"Okay," I said.

The Oracle watched me for a few moments, before her black wings appeared, and she took off into the sky.

She left me alone in the thick grass.

Well, alone except for Caliya, who rubbed her head against my stomach, wanting attention.

I laughed as I stroked the tiger's fur, bringing my hand up to her ear, petting her calmly.

Being with Caliya made me incredibly happy, it made me feel like I was doing what I was destined to do.

Be the Protector of the Earth.

To trust nature.

I loved my abilities so much.

But I also had to save Viro and Thera, after all they had gone through. Save them *again*.

There was suddenly so much that I had to do, but I knew, somewhere in my gut, that I was the only one who could do this.

But Celio would help me, along with some other Beings and Creatures, both from the Earth, and from the Afterworld.

And I would be ready.

I was ready for my journey to the Heavens.

I ran my hands over my braid; I was sitting in the treehouse staring at myself in the mirror.

A mirror that was from the Ethereal City; my father had brought it down when he'd named me the Protector of the Earth.

Caliya was beside me, rumbling softly, as I watched myself in the reflective glass.

My blue-tinted blond hair. My peacock feather tattoos which spread to the sides of my eyes. But the hesitant look etched on my face radiated throughout my entire body.

I was nervous; it was evident in my body language.

Caliya seemed to pick up on my emotions; she pushed her body into mine, distracting me immediately as her tail swatted the air. Happy rumbles escaped her throat as I petted her ears.

Oh, Caliya, I thought. *You are too sweet.*

I scratched under her chin, which instantly made her eyes close in contentment. I chuckled as her tail swatted the air once more.

Aww, Caliya. I'm going to miss you, sweetheart. I'll be back, though.

I had to face yet another threat to the Realms, and, for right now, leave the tiger behind. But I would be back.

I would return to my home; the Earth. The treehouse in which I sat in now.

There would be peace again, and I would make that happen.

I was the Protector of the Earth, and I would guard the Realm I called home, along with the others.

I can do this.

Caliya's throaty rumble made me turn my head.

She'd wandered over to the window of the treehouse. Her amber eyes were focused, her tail still.

I blinked.

She was watching something in the fading light.

I shook my head.

It wasn't just anything that she was looking at; I knew, in a heartbeat, who it was.

"No, Caliya. No," I said automatically. Only afterward, I was greeted outside by a snort, and then a whinny.

A grin spread across my face as I heard the Winged Horse outside. I walked over and saw Maximus.

I gasped.

He appeared to be even more muscular, larger than he had been before, when we had embarked on the trek to defeat Thana.

The Winged Horse was magnificent, and he knew it.

I smiled at the sight of him. I walked out of the treehouse with Caliya following me. I glanced down at her; her amber eyes were fixed on Maximus.

He looked warily at her, his snout going high in the air, his wings beginning to flap as he got agitated.

I looked down at Caliya. "No, Caliya. No," I said, repeating myself from before. "No."

The tigress looked up at me before lying down on the grass, listening to my words.

I leaned over and petted her mammoth head one last time.

"Alright, sweetie. Be good, Caliya."

Now, I had to begin my journey, leaving her behind.

I sighed, glancing up at Maximus.

The Winged Horse snorted, turning his head toward me before I approached him, petting his neck.

I stroked his fur calmly, and he bowed low so I could get on him.

I did so, running my fingers through part of his mane, and grasped it tightly.

The black stallion nickered before rearing again, extending his wings.

I held on as he took off, galloping across the green grass. The wind whipped around, going straight in my face; he was going so fast I thought that I was already flying.

After a few moments of Maximus picking up enough speed, the Winged Horse was airborne and going into the atmosphere with me along for the ride.

Going to the Afterworld, the World Beyond, where I would be starting a brand-new, but dangerous, trek.

This was going to be interesting.

I gripped Maximus' mane tightly as he flew through the clouds, making his way into the Heavens.

He flapped his wings every so often as he went against the air gusts, but I wasn't scared as we flew up to the World Beyond.

I had a task to do, and I was ready for it.

The breeze whipped through my hair as I held on tight to the ink-black Winged Horse, as he navigated his way carefully through the clouds.

The clouds that would lead to the Afterworld.

I held on tight to Maximus as he neared the Heavens.

He climbed higher and higher until we weren't in the clouds anymore… We were so far up that we were *above* them.

The surroundings were still the sky, only now that it was nighttime on Earth, the Heavens were beginning to copy the way everything looked.

Almost a twilight color with a faded blue undertone.

Faded blue and beautiful.

I felt when the Winged Horse had reached the Afterworld. He'd begun to slow down.

I stayed as calm as I could as Maximus threw his wings back; he was rearing up in order to slow down, even though we were still high in the sky.

I just held on to his mane as he prepared to land, and within moments, his hind hooves hit a gigantic cloud-like substance.

A substance that was not like the Earth.

A grin spread across my face as Maximus brought his front hooves down.

He slowed to a trot once he was on the Heavenly surface.

He flapped his wings as soon as he landed, bringing them up and extending them as high as he could before neighing.

I laughed, bringing my hands across his neck, petting him.

"You are a great Winged Horse, Maximus," I told him.

He nickered at me, and I smiled. The Winged Horse knew that he was majestic.

"Can I get down, please?" I asked him, and immediately he bowed low, allowing me to dismount.

I slid off Maximus easily, hitting the surface before I walked over to the horse's head.

I ran my hands over Maximus' muzzle, instantly calming him.

He nickered softly once more, rubbing his head against my side.

I laughed, absorbed in petting the Winged Horse, when a voice caught my attention.

"Chrysanthe?"

My heartrate climbed at just the mention of my name, that familiar tone...

I turned around, my hand still on the Winged Horse's snout; a soft nicker erupted from him yet again as I saw Celio.

Celio.

My love who was also the Guardian of the Spirits, the Protector of the Afterworld.

He smiled as he advanced toward me; I grinned back.

His body was strong and defined underneath the white shirt he wore; my eyes followed him as he came closer to me.

Celio appeared to have come out of a castle that seemed to be floating in the air.

Well built, strong, and sturdy.

Towering above the both of us, the castle went way past where I could see when I looked up.

It was a very special place.

It was the Home of the Archangels in Heaven.

"Hi," I greeted Celio, bringing my attention back to him.

Celio came to my side, putting his hand on Maximus' neck, and then gazed into my face; a soft smile was still on his lips.

"Hi," he said back, his hazel eyes latching onto mine. "Is Maximus treating you well?"

He was still petting the Winged Horse as he spoke.

I grinned. "Yes. Yes, he's been a great steed."

I glanced over at the equine, running my hands between his ears, over the piece of his mane. He rubbed his head into my abdomen.

Another laugh made its way through my throat.

"He seems to like you," Celio mused; I just smiled at my love.

"You are too sweet, Maximus," I told the stallion, before I pet him one last time.

Then I twisted toward Celio, who was watching me steadily.

He blinked as he looked at me, and then he glanced at our surroundings-the pure white of the Afterworld.

He motioned around the World Beyond, and automatically, I knew he wanted to show me his Realm.

I nodded, and we both walked away from Maximus. The stallion snorted, reared up, and flew off.

I turned as I saw him take off; Celio just chuckled. I looked at the Archangel, who was amused.

"He always needs to show off," he said.

"I guess so," I responded, smiling back at him.

I sighed, my attention on Celio, and then spoke again.

"Sybella sent me Maximus; she said that there was danger in the Ethereal City. A Being from Hell, as well as a Minotaur that has been unleashed. They both are terrorizing the City. Sybella said I needed to get here, to the Afterworld, by nightfall."

I paused, and saw Celio nod at my words.

"She said you had seen the Being and the Minotaur; that you were the one who told her."

Celio nodded once more. "Yes, that is true, Chrysanthe. Somehow, the Hell Being has gotten into the City, and brought the Minotaur with him. I immediately told the Oracle as soon as I saw her."

Celio sighed. "I'm glad you're safe," he said, his gaze locked on me.

I grinned, leaning forward, and kissed his cheek.

"I missed you," I told him. He just stared at me for a moment, when there was an abrupt whistle in the distance.

Celio and I both looked up at the same time, and then I grinned in surprise.

That was because there were two Archangels in the distance.

Two Archangels that I hadn't seen in millennia, since I had first met Celio, before I became the Protector of the Earth.

Both smiled at Celio and I. They approached us, a happy expression on their faces.

One Archangel was male, while the other was female.

Brother and sister.

"Well, hello," the male said to me. "Long time."

"Nice to see you again, Chrysanthe," the female said as she stood beside her brother.

"Nice to see you too," I responded.

They were going to help me defeat the threat. I knew this instinctively. The brother and sister would help me, as well as Celio.

I wouldn't be alone.

he Archangels approached us with grins on their faces. They stopped right in front of Celio and I, and I couldn't help but smile back.

I hadn't seen Beacon and Nevaeh in millennia, and now they were right in front of me.

Beacon had dark hair and blue eyes, while his sister had the same features.

Nevaeh had a yellow dress on that resembled sunlight, while Beacon wore a blue shirt that was a little darker than the sky on an illuminated, healthy day.

Beacon represented truth, confidence, and Heaven; Nevaeh represented hope, light, and happiness.

Both Archangels were the same in their way of thinking, but they were different as well.

The colors of their clothing were unique, but they had eclectic meanings.

I blinked before I looked at Beacon and Nevaeh, smiling at them once more.

"How are you?" I asked them both.

Beacon shrugged, while Nevaeh glanced at her brother for a split moment; she turned and met my eyes.

She shook her head, biting her lip.

"We're not doing that well, Chrysanthe. The Being from Hell, he's not only trying to destroy the Ethereal City... he threatened the Heavens as well. Beacon and I, we already lost two Archangel friends to the Phantom. One was caught by the Phantom's messenger and later trapped in the Abyss. He was eaten by the Minotaur. The other one was found by the Phantom and had her Fate Tattoos torn out; she had her wings ripped off."

Nevaeh paused, gathering herself together again; she spoke once more.

"We thought we had lost another friend when Celio was torn from the Afterworld."

Her eyes met Celio's, who'd stayed silent the entire conversation out of respect.

He just watched her as she talked.

"We didn't lose him though," Neveah continued.

She twisted her attention to me.

"Chrysanthe," she said, staring at me. "Chrysanthe, the reason the Phantom tore Celio out of the Afterworld was because she knew he was, *is*, your love."

I blinked, glancing over at Celio, who automatically gritted his teeth; his jaw was tight.

I had never known that.

My eyes met Nevaeh's, complete shock on my face.

We stared at each other for a moment before Beacon interjected.

"Nevaeh and I, we don't want to lose any more friends. Archangels or Celestial Beings, to be exact."

His voice was a little shaky, but then he cleared his throat, and spoke again.

"Chrysanthe, we need you to vanquish the Minotaur, as well as Acanthus. They are both dangerously close to eliminating all the Celestial Beings in the Ethereal City, and the Archangels here."

Beacon swallowed; he then finished what he was saying.

"Chrysanthe, you are the only one who can save us all."

I inhaled deeply, exhaling slowly as I quickly saw all eyes on me. Celio, Beacon, and Nevaeh.

It's okay, Chrysanthe. It's okay. I can do this. I can do this, I thought as Neveah watched me.

I kept repeating those words in my skull; Neveah spoke up, interrupting my thoughts.

"You won't be alone. You will have help to vanquish the Minotaur and Acanthus. But only *you*," she put emphasis on that last word, "can rid the World of these dangers."

Words spoken exactly like Sybella.

I gulped before I nodded.

"Alright," I said, holding her stare. "Okay, I can do this."

I pulled my eyes away from Nevaeh, instead glancing over at Celio.

He nodded slightly as I looked into his eyes, and I felt the tight wad of nervousness in my gut dissipate.

Celio gazed at me encouragingly.

I brought my attention back to the female Archangel.

"Sybella didn't say what to do after meeting up with Celio," I told Nevaeh. "She just said I would receive help from other Beings and Archangels. She didn't specify, though."

"That's because it would be a lot to take in," Beacon said; I turned my attention to him.

"This quest to save the Realms is even bigger and more dangerous than when you went up against the Queen of Death."

I swallowed, and then Beacon went on.

"Nevaeh and I will be your guides through this journey, pointing you in the right direction so you know who to speak with and what to do."

Beacon glanced at his sister, who was still beside him; she met his gaze, and then she brought her attention to me.

"Chrysanthe, the most important Being that you are going to see throughout this trek is Phoenix. He is in the Ethereal City at the current moment," she said, and my heartrate quickened.

Phoenix. Phoenix. The oldest Celestial Being in existence.

The shapeshifting Being who also taught the Oracle.

I'd heard about him from Sybella, but I'd never met him before. I looked at Nevaeh.

"Maximus will help you go to the Ethereal City so you can meet Phoenix," she said. "The only thing that you need to know, is that in order to receive help from Phoenix, you must do something for him. You need to help him first."

I nodded understandingly.

"Okay," I said.

Phoenix was the oldest Being in existence, so everything that Nevaeh had just said made sense.

If I would help him, he would help me.

"That is the second part of your journey, Chrysanthe," Nevaeh stated. "To get an item for Phoenix first."

hoenix.

The shapeshifting Being who had been the Oracle's mentor.

Now, I had to get an item for him.

The oldest Celestial Being in existence, Phoenix was obviously extremely powerful, and, because he was the oldest Being ever, he specialized in spells and enchantments.

At least, that was what I was told by Sybella.

Beacon just watched me as the thoughts spun around inside my head.

"I know that this is a lot to take in," he said, turning to me. "You can, you *must*, do this. The Heaven's fate is in your hands, Chrysanthe."

I gulped before I looked over at Celio.

His hazel eyes gripping mine somehow gave me the strength I needed.

All hesitation and doubt in myself melted away as I met his gaze.

"When do I have to leave?" I asked.

It was Nevaeh who answered.

"By the end of two nights here," she said. "By the beginning of the third morning, you must go to the Aerial Alpines. After that, you can go to the Ethereal City to see Phoenix. Maximus, he knows the way, so there is no confusion as to where to go. The Winged Horse will get you there."

Nevaeh looked at Celio.

"Celio," she said, "you can go with her, but you *must* be careful. Beacon and I already lost you once; we don't want to lose you again."

Celio looked at the siblings, nodding silently.

"Well, we all figured you could use some rest after coming here," Nevaeh said. "It seems like you're tired from the trip to the Heavens."

I nodded.

It was true.

I was exhausted. My eyelids were drooping; I could barely keep them open.

"Well, Beacon and I will be showing you a spare room in the Divine Castle," she said.

I nodded, and a few moments later, I yawned.

The sky was darkening fast, the color almost turning ink-black.

"Alright," Nevaeh said, glancing over at Beacon and then looking at me. "Well then, Chrysanthe, welcome to the Afterworld."

I followed Beacon and Nevaeh as they walked into the Divine Castle, glancing every so often at Nevaeh's yellow dress.

It was beautiful, the color of sunlight, and the back of it was partly lace and see-through until the fabric got to her hips.

It was when the clothing hit a certain portion of her body that it was solid again.

The back of her dress exposed her wings, her Fate Tattoo, black and gorgeous on her silky skin.

I brought my attention back to my surroundings as we all walked into the Home of the Archangels.

I was taken aback by what I saw inside.

The interior of the Divine Castle was gargantuan; there were many rooms, windows, and doors throughout the gigantic floating residence.

The entire place was enormous. I followed Beacon and Nevaeh, with Celio by my side.

I was unable to speak because I was in awe of the Home of the Archangels.

Celio stayed with me as I walked over the carpets that were in the hallways. I took a glance over at him, who just gave me a soft smile and a wink.

I smiled back, before my eyes shifted over at Nevaeh, who had turned around to look at me.

We'd reached a room down a long hallway.

Nevaeh met my eyes as I stopped in front of her; Beacon opened the ornate door as his sister gestured toward the inside of it.

"This is your room, Chrysanthe," she said, stepping into the massive bedchamber.

I went into the area, and then paused, glancing around.

There was a huge window on the side of the space; it allowed anyone to see the atmosphere, the Heavenly surroundings.

A unique carpet covered the floor and a large bed was in the middle of the expanse, taking up a large portion of the room.

Before I lived permanently on Earth, I'd lived in the Ethereal City. The Home of the Archangels reminded me of my original home, where I was born.

I blinked a few times, bringing my thoughts back to the present; I looked at Nevaeh, who'd been watching my reaction.

"It's beautiful," I said to her. "Thank you so much for this."

Nevaeh smiled.

"You're welcome, Chrysanthe. You need a nice place to stay while you wait to go to the Ethereal City. I'll leave you alone now," she said. I'd yawned, abruptly feeling exhausted.

I nodded sleepily.

"Okay, well, I will see you in the morning then," I said, glancing over at Beacon and Nevaeh.

I yawned once more. The sibling Archangels then turned around, opened the door, and left the bedroom.

I glanced over at Celio as Beacon and Nevaeh walked away. Their footsteps receded from the area.

Celio watched me as my eyelids started to get heavy, and then leaned toward me, kissing my cheek.

Even though I was groggy, my left cheek instantly felt warm.

I smiled at him.

"Goodnight, Chrysanthe," his breath tickled the pores in my skin.

A soft smile was on his lips as he stared at me. I nodded at my love, and then Celio turned around, walking to the ornate entrance of the bedroom.

He opened it, glancing at me for one last moment. He walked out afterward, shutting the door.

I heard his footsteps as he advanced down the hallway, before I yawned, exhaustion taking over me.

I'd found some clothing to sleep in before I went over to the bed.

I pulled back the cover, collapsing into the sheets.

I was asleep almost instantly.

I slowly opened my eyes, blinking away the sleep.

The sunlight streamed in, and for a moment, I forgot where I was.

It was only after I saw the gigantic, open window that I remembered I was in the Heavens.

I smiled as I threw my arms above my head, stretching, and then climbed out from underneath the covers.

I grabbed some clothes from the closet, changing quickly, and then gazed at my reflection in a mirror nearby.

The dress fit me perfectly, but my hair was falling out of the braid. I sighed, studying my appearance, and then I walked over to the door and opened it, making my way down the hallway.

"Chrysanthe?"

I heard Celio say my name as I walked into the living room.

A grin spread across my face as I looked up to see Celio nearing me.

Another white shirt covered his body. He appeared healthy and strong.

He came over, giving me a warm hug.

"Good morning, Chrysanthe," he said softly, pulling away from me to gaze at my face.

"Good morning, Celio," I responded, my voice a whisper as we watched each other.

Celio's hazel eyes seemed to burn into mine as he stared at me. He pulled me close, bringing his lips to mine gently.

My heart was pummeling my ribcage, and then Celio backed away from me, staring at me steadily.

I grinned at him before I heard footsteps coming from a nearby room.

Celio and I both looked up as Nevaeh made her way over. She had a new dress on. Now, she had a purple one.

A stunning, deep color that reminded me of my mother's dress.

"Hello, Chrysanthe, and Celio," Nevaeh said, glancing at the both of us. "Chrysanthe, I hope you slept well. Were you comfortable?" she asked, to which I nodded.

"Yes. Yes, I was," I replied.

"Good. That is great to hear," Nevaeh said.

She looked at Celio and I, and nodded.

"That is great to hear," she repeated. "I will get Beacon, and he can tell you what you must do in the Aerial Alpines, Chrysanthe."

I nodded.

Nevaeh smiled before she left the room, her purple dress shimmering as she walked.

The dress was made of the same fabric and layout as the yellow one, the only difference being the color; Nevaeh's Fate Tattoos were showing as she turned back around, away from Celio and I.

I watched her leave, my eyes focusing on her black wings that were inked on her skin. I saw Nevaeh turn a corner in the Divine Castle, and that was when I couldn't see her anymore.

I sighed, looking over at Celio, who just smiled.

"Whatever happens, I'll be with you, Chrysanthe."

He kissed my cheek.

There was a tight knot in my stomach, but Celio pulled me into a hug, and the uncomfortable feeling dissipated.

"I'll be with you," Celio breathed into my ear. "I always will."

Footsteps on the carpet made me turn my head.

My eyes met Beacon's as he walked beside his sister.

Both of them stopped in front of Celio and I. I inhaled slowly, and that was when I felt Celio's warm hand in mine. I glanced at him, and saw him holding my gaze.

He was going to be with me, no matter what happened.

Beacon sighed, before he spoke.

"Chrysanthe, by the end of two nights here, you must go to the Aerial Alpines. As Nevaeh told you, you will need to leave tomorrow morning. Maximus will know the way, so there is no need to worry. Chrysanthe, you must get a Fire Ruby, to help Phoenix regain his power. He is consistently morphing and the Ruby will restore Phoenix's ability, as well as strengthen him. He is, after all, the most important Being that you will meet on this journey."

I nodded. "Okay," I said, taking in the information. "Is there a special place for the Ruby?"

"Yes," Beacon answered. "It is in a cave in the Aerial Alpines, guarded by the Aureate Doe. The deer is very special to a Celestial Being, named Cyra. You will have to talk to her as well. Maximus will know exactly where to go."

Aerial Alpines. Fire Ruby. The Aureate Doe. Cyra the Celestial Being.

I nodded absently as I absorbed his words. I needed to go to the Aerial Alpines, get a Fire Ruby from Cyra, and then go to the Ethereal City.

Of course, I would have Celio with me as well.

My heart was thudding my ribs as I looked at Beacon, and then took a half glance at Nevaeh, who stared at me.

I knew what both Archangels were thinking. They wanted to make sure that I knew the task.

"Go to the Aerial Alpines, get the Fire Ruby from the Aureate Doe and Cyra, and then go see Phoenix."

Beacon and Nevaeh both nodded.

"Okay, Chrysanthe," Beacon said. "Now, there are many Beings you will meet throughout your journey, and both Nevaeh and I," he paused, peering at his sister, "both of us would like you to meet Hali. She is the water sprite who Guards the Heavenly Falls. We would like you to meet her before tomorrow morning, since she will help you on another portion of this journey."

"Okay," I said.

"Are you ready to leave? Nevaeh and I wanted to go to the Heavenly Falls right now."

"Yes," I told him. "Yes, I'm ready."

And then I was following Beacon and Nevaeh, with Celio beside me.

We were going to see the water sprite, the Guardian of the Heavenly Falls.

I was going to meet Hali.

10

Acanthus

My natural green eyes stared back at me as I looked in the mirror. I seethed, feeling like my blood was going to boil as I took in my reflection.

My muscles tensed as I threw my arms out, against the nearby wall. I shook as anger ripped through my body, and my inhale scraped through my teeth.

I leaned against the wall, bringing my eyes down to the carpet, trying to calm myself, but it didn't work as I turned and looked at the mirror once more.

My black shirt was tattered, while my eyes appeared venomous. My Fate Tattoos wound around both of my arms. They appeared to be suffocating them, the vines and thorns creeping up my flesh to both of my shoulders. My black hair partly went into my eyes as I glared.

A yell ripped through my throat; I threw my right arm out, punching the wall.

The force of the movement broke through it, but I couldn't feel the pain.

All I could feel was the anger festering inside me.

Anger, at Viro and Thera, for rejecting their own flesh and blood. Anger at Chrysanthe, for sending Thana back to the Underworld for all eternity.

But most of all, I was angry with myself.

Angry since I could've stopped Chrysanthe. I could have stopped Thana from being sent back to Hell. I could've saved Thana.

A mixture between a sob and a growl erupted from my throat, and I blinked away angry tears. I should've... I should've...

I was a shapeshifter; I could change into whatever Being or animal I wanted. I should've been able to save her...

"UGH!" I screamed, bringing my fist back before punching the wall once more.

"Hello?"

I blinked when I heard a Being right outside in the hallway. I looked up, but that was when I heard a knock on the bedchamber door.

"Hello? Who is in here?"

I immediately backed up into the middle of the room, before I hit the edge of the bed.

The sound of the door opening made my skin crawl, but I knew exactly what to do.

My muscles tensed as I abruptly shrank, and I grew eight legs, skittering away right as the Being walked in. I made my way from her as she just blinked, looking throughout the bedchamber.

She didn't realize that I was the spider in the corner of the room, just waiting for her to go away.

I did notice her eyes go wide as she noticed the hole in the wall.

She stared for a few moments, and then her eyes darted around the room. She finally walked out of the bedchamber, shaking her head.

I waited a few moments, waited until her footsteps receded, and then I shifted back into my Being self.

I breathed deeply, and then I opened my eyes, only to peer around the massive bedchamber. The place that used to belong to the King and Queen of all Celestials.

Viro and Thera.

I'd gotten in here by shapeshifting into an insect and crawling underneath the door. I'd been sorting through the entire chamber, seeing if there was anything of value. Anything to steal. I'd been in here for the entire morning, climbing all around the chamber since there were a lot of objects and items on the carpeted floor.

The massive bedchamber though, it hadn't been cleaned for several seasons. Either the Beings here were scared to clean it, or it was just left untouched on purpose. Either way, the room was filthy.

Everything was gathering dust, since Viro and Thera were no longer in the Ethereal City. Which made it easy to enter.

I peered around the room, taking my surroundings in. There was a mirror on the wall, propped up against it, while the bedsheets were dusty. No one had been in here for quite a while. I looked into the mirror once more, watching myself, before I spotted an object in the reflective glass. I turned to see a baby cradle beside the bed.

"What the...?"

I trailed off as I walked over, wiping away the dust.

My heart was pounding, and I held the cradle in both hands as I inspected the object.

It was all pitch black, and I ran my thumb over the carvings that were in it. The material the cradle was made of was very weak. It was weathered down since it had been unused. I was still careful as I watched it.

There was just something about this item...

I looked around the bedchamber, glancing at everything.

This area was abandoned. No one was going to be, or had used, this chamber for a long time. Which meant that I could steal anything of value from Viro and Thera. This room was already collecting dust; no one was going to *really* clean it.

I might as well just take what I want, I thought.

I looked around the area, seeing if there was anything of value. I kept the baby bed in my line of sight, though. I didn't want to lose that object.

I sorted through Viro's belongings. I was stealing whatever seemed the most valuable, as well as the most sentimental. I was sorting through both Viro and Thera's possessions.

Basically, anything they had loved, I took it from their bedchamber.

I caught sight of the mirror once more. My hair was ink-black, while my eyes were a venomous green. My normally peach colored skin was filthy, smeared with dust and dirt.

The Fate Tattoos covered both my arms, but they appeared to be cutting the blood flow in my extremities. My tattoos were ominous; Hell tattoos.

I stared at them, before moving my eyes to look at my face in the mirror.

My eyes almost appeared reptilian, while my natural body was strong.

Strong enough to handle me shapeshifting consistently.

I felt my skin beginning to quiver and crawl, and I shifted into an Archangel. I suddenly had brown hair and blue eyes, while my clothing restored itself.

The black shirt was repaired as I saw sunlight streaming through the window.

I gazed at my now Archangel features, grinning. I loved being able to shapeshift.

I turned around to see a window, but that was when I caught sight of something. Something on the other side of the bed.

I walked over, and realized it was another baby cradle. It had a blue-green color to it, and I ran my fingers over the material, getting rid of the dust. That was when I saw that there was a name engraved on it.

So beautiful, so clean in the way it was done, that I had to swallow the bile that crept up in my throat.

The lettering was in gold.

The cradle said: *Chrysanthe.*

It took me a few moments for me to understand, but when it hit me, I was furious. My hands were shaking violently, but I also felt like my head was going to explode.

I twisted around to see the other cradle in my line of sight. The other baby bed was completely black. No carved letters at all.

No wonder Thana had hated her sister. Thana got nothing from anyone, especially her parents.

Meanwhile, Chrysanthe was on Earth, protecting it, getting all the admiration.

Chrysanthe got everything, and Thana got nothing.

My hands trembled as I gritted my teeth together. Finally, I picked up the cradle and threw it with all my strength against the mirror. Both shattered into tiny pieces.

I ignored the sound of the glass and baby cradle breaking, and that was when I turned around to see the window.

I must get out of here. I must get out of here...

I yanked the window up just in time to hear frantic footsteps coming toward the door.

Within moments, my fake black wings came out of my back. Then I took off, flying away into the open air, leaving Viro and Thera's bedchamber behind.

11

Chrysanthe

Nevaeh, Beacon, and Celio were right; the Heavenly Falls, the location was absolutely stunning.

The waterfall was gorgeous, while the liquid was turquoise-blue. The rocks were gray.

The Heavenly Falls, they were also colorful, since the sun had scattered illumination all over the area.

Everything was sparkling and had different variations of hues.

It was all so breathtaking, the way the Waters looked.

A smile spread across my face as I saw the lively surroundings around me; I turned toward Celio, who was holding me in his arms.

His pulse was against my skin, and I brought my left hand up to his neck as he looked at me with his hazel eyes.

Celio had flown me up to the Falls.

Beacon, Nevaeh, and Celio could obviously fly, since they were Archangels.

I didn't have that ability, nor did I have the Fate Tattoo to do so.

So, Celio had flown with me in his arms to the enchanted Falls.

He looked at me, and I slid my chrysanthemum-tattooed hand to the back of his neck, pulling him toward me so his mouth met mine.

I could feel my heartbeat against my ribs, and I backed away, feeling Celio's breath against my skin, sinking into my pores.

Just that sensation made my insides squirm as he gazed at me, his eyes like liquid gold…

The sounds of the waterfall filled my ears as Celio and I watched each other, and I was automatically reminded of when we had gone on the trek to defeat Thana.

The Enchanted Cascades….

Celio and I had both jumped into the Waters, getting clean in order to not attract the wrong kind of attention.

Celio and I were in the Enchanted Cascades…

It had been just the two of us.

Alone.

I felt a blush rise in my cheeks as the memory took over, and I noticed Celio squint.

He glanced at the Heavenly Falls for about two moments, and then looked back at me.

He raised his eyebrows, before a seductive smile appeared on his mouth.

"Is this Water reminding you of anything?" Celio asked, breathing into my lips, making me feel intoxicated.

I nodded automatically, staring at his eyes, before kissing him again.

Celio's embrace was so warm; he was holding me so tight… His lips were so soft…

My heart pummeled my ribs so hard I thought they would get bruised… But then I broke away from Celio, knowing there were others waiting on us.

Beacon, Nevaeh, and the water sprite named Hali.

Celio let me go, setting me down on the hard rock when he got to the top of the Heavenly Falls, where Beacon and Nevaeh were waiting.

I grinned at Celio, still feeling his hands around my waist as I turned to Nevaeh, who was to the left of me.

Beacon was on my right.

Once I got my bearings, Celio's limbs receded from my skin. I smiled at him again before turning to Nevaeh, who had a small stone in her hand.

She gently tossed the rock into the Water, and it skipped across the liquid.

Nevaeh grinned widely, before calling out, "Hali!"

I blinked, looking into the fluid, and then I saw a multicolored figure within the depths.

Yellow, green, and blue.

The figure moved quickly, and then I saw it swim to the middle of the pool.

Within moments, long blond hair appeared from beneath the small waves. A pink starfish was on the corner of the sprite's mane, while I saw mixed colors on her wings.

Purple and teal hues adorned her back, while the yellows, greens, and blues covered her front and neck. They covered her sun-kissed skin, and a sand dollar necklace rested on her heart. She also had a seaweed top that went over her chest.

Seashell tattoos covered Hali's arms as she slowly made herself visible, and I smiled.

"Hello, Hali," Nevaeh said, grinning warmly at the water sprite.

Hali had a happy expression on her face as she looked at us. Her turquoise eyes sparkled from the sunlight, which danced along the Heavenly Falls. A tattoo of an orange-red octopus rested on her neck, spreading across her throat, and spilling slightly over her chest.

Hali glanced at all of us, and then brought her attention back to Nevaeh.

"Hello, Nevaeh," Hali said as she rose completely out of the Water.

She had blue fabric on the bottom half of her frame, slightly worn from being in the fluid. Everything that she wore, including her Fate Tattoo, glistened in the sunlight.

Hali looked at Nevaeh, and then at Beacon, Celio, and I.

She blinked as her eyes went on mine, and then her gaze shifted once to Celio. Then Hali looked back at me.

"Hello, Chrysanthe," she said, watching me. "Hello, Celio," she said, turning her head toward him. Hali blinked once more, but then she twisted to Nevaeh again.

The Archangel spoke to Hali. "Beacon and I wanted Chrysanthe to meet you. The Oracle- as well as Beacon, Celio, and I- have all told Chrysanthe about the terror going on in the Ethereal City. We have also all agreed to help her. I figured that she could meet you before she goes to the Aerial Alpines."

Hali nodded. "And meet me, you will," she said, watching my eyes. "There are many Beings coming together to help you, Chrysanthe. But, as you probably already know, you must be the one to *defeat* the threat. Only *you* can do this. You *must.*" She pleaded.

I gulped, but then felt a hand on my arm.

"It's alright," Celio whispered to me.

I sucked in a breath, attempting to calm myself.

I knew I had to defeat the threat on my own, Sybella had told me that. The words Hali were saying though, they made me feel anxious. Sybella was the first Being to tell me this, but now that I heard it from another, it made everything seem so real.

I gulped. I took a deep breath before clearing my throat.

"How can… how can you help, Hali?"

The sprite looked into my eyes. "I can help you find a very precious weapon. One that can defeat the Minotaur, as well as Acanthus. It is buried deep within the depths of this body of water," she said. "Both of you," Hali stated, looking at me, and then at

Celio. "Both of you are scarred from Thana. I can help heal you, but you must kill the Minotaur. Using the blood of the Minotaur, along with both of yours, will unlock the Falls for you. Right now, I protect the Falls, but once I have what I need, I will assist you."

I nodded at her words, before she continued.

"I will help you, but the very first thing to do is fly up to the Aerial Alpines. There you will find the Fire Ruby that will help Phoenix. You don't need my help now, but I will assist when the moment comes."

I nodded once more, absorbing her words.

Inside though, I felt incredibly anxious. This was going to be the hardest thing to do in my entire existence.

But I felt fingertips brush against my arm, and I knew that Celio could sense my uneasiness.

"I'll be with you, don't worry," he breathed, and I turned to face him. He had a calm expression as our eyes met, and he wrapped his arm around my body, pulling me toward him. "Everything is going to be okay."

"It was nice to meet you, Chrysanthe," Hali said, causing me to turn toward her. She looked at Beacon and Nevaeh, with a last glance at Celio. "It was nice to see you three again. I must get back to the Heavenly Falls now, but I will help Chrysanthe when she completes the first task."

I peered into her eyes. "Go to the Aerial Alpines and get the Fire Ruby for Phoenix."

Hali nodded. "Exactly."

I watched as she then twisted around; she disappeared into the vastness of the Heavenly Falls. She left all four of us, leaving small bubbles in her wake.

12

Acanthus

I was seething as I made my way out of the Ethereal City, my fake wings pushing me higher and higher into the atmosphere.

I just needed to get away. I needed to leave.

Seeing the baby cradles just made my blood boil.

The fact that nobody cared about Thana... No one looked out for her...

I gritted my teeth together at the thought.

Thana had been abandoned and had drowned in the Inferno River, the body of liquid that led to the Underworld, to Hell.

She'd been left to die...

I snarled as I continued to fly away from the Ethereal City, but then an idea struck me.

The Inferno River, it led to the Underworld.

Not far from the Inferno River was a swamp. A swamp where the Seer Sisters lived.

The Seer Sisters could tell the future, and the Beings, named Levana and Morana, were blind. Blind, except when they had a bull skull headpiece they would take turns wearing.

Whenever they weren't wearing the skull, their eyes would become milky. Milky and clouded.

The Being would become blind once more.

The Inferno River came into view as I threw my wings out, landing on the soft, squishy ground.

I saw one of the Seer Sisters poke her head out of the tent in which they lived. Her eyes were clouded and white.

She grasped her sister's hand, fumbling for the bull skull.

"Morana," I heard the seer say. "Morana, I hear something. Give me the skull."

Morana's extremity poked out of the tent, before she positioned the animal skull on Levana's head.

Immediately, Levana's eyes were showing. Green eyes with a black pupil in the center.

She had on a long, black robe, while Morana had dull, faded brown robes. They both had long brown hair in eclectic braids, and long black fingernails. Dark ink covered both Levana and Morana's eyes, making them look formidable.

Tattoos of animal skulls covered both of their arms.

Since Levana and Morana were seers and could say what the future would hold, that meant a sacrifice, or blood as payment.

The bull skull that was on Levana's head was bewitched so that the seers' vision would come back whenever it was on their head.

Both sisters came out from the tent; Morana was completely blind, while Levana just stopped and looked at me.

I quickly realized as I stared at her that I still appeared to be an Archangel. I abruptly felt my skin crawl as I morphed back into myself. My wings disappeared, and I saw Levana blink.

She watched me for a moment before she spoke.

"You wish to know the future, don't you?" Levana asked, stepping forward. "Is it that you want to go back to the Underworld once again?"

The wind picked up as she took a step closer. It blew through the swamp, the Seer Sister's robes.

I nodded at Levana.

"Well, Acanthus, knowledge demands payment," she stated.

"If you don't have payment, we cannot tell you anything," Morana interjected.

Morana was right beside her sister, clutching Levana's arm blindly.

Levana glanced over at her sibling, before she looked over at me. "Acanthus," Levana said. "Do you have payment?"

I nodded, and then glanced down at my pockets. I'd stolen a few things when I was in Viro and Thera's bedchamber.

A few gold coins with a Winged Horse imprinted on the back, and a griffon feather.

I pulled out the objects as Levana stared.

"Morana," she said while watching me. "Morana, go get the knife from inside the tent."

Levana gave the bewitched animal skull to her sister, placing it on her head before Morana went inside. I clutched the items in my hand.

It was only a few moments later when Morana returned, a sharp knife with her.

She looked at Levana, who was now blind.

"Levana," Morana said. "Hold out your palm, I'm giving you the knife."

Morana touched Levana's arm as Levana held her palm straight out. She carefully gave Levana the handle of the weapon. Then she took the bull skull off her head, instead giving it to her sister.

Morana's green eyes instantly faded and became clouded as Levana's became visible.

Levana instantly looked down at the sharp object in her palm. She gripped the handle, and glanced at me. She brought her gaze to my extremity that was holding the objects. She looked at them curiously, trying to see if what I had was of any real value.

"Where did you find these items, Acanthus?"

Levana stared at my hands for a few moments, and then brought her gaze back up to me.

"Viro and Thera's bedchamber," I said. "I was sorting through their belongings earlier."

Levana nodded approvingly. She then said, "Hold out your hand, Acanthus, palm up."

I did what she told me; I moved the objects to my right extremity as my left was extended in front of Levana. I knew what was going to happen next as she brought the sharp knife into my line of sight. She positioned it over my left palm.

Abruptly, Levana sliced through my open hand.

I sucked in a breath at the pain, but then I saw Levana looking over at Morana; Levana quickly took the bull skull and put it on her sister's head.

Morana blinked as her sight came back, and then her sibling spoke to her.

"Morana, go get cloth from inside the tent."

The seer looked at her sister blindly, before Morana disappeared.

I winced at the ache in my palm as blood pooled in it, but right when I was going to say something, Morana came back.

She had a long cloth in one hand, and some bottled liquid in the other.

I watched her as she wrapped my wounded palm in the fabric, before taking the objects from my other hand. I sucked in a breath as I saw the cloth instantly become soaked in red.

The cloth was on me for a few moments before Morana took it off my palm. She lifted it from my skin, and put the liquid from the bottle on the wound.

At first, there was a stinging sensation, then a cooling one. After the cool feeling, I realized the slice in my palm had completely healed. All that was left was a scar.

I looked at Morana, who had the objects in her hand. She had the bloody cloth in one palm, and the items in another.

Morana looked over at her sister, gingerly placing the cloth in her hand. Then she placed the bull skull on Levana's head.

Levana immediately looked down as soon as her sight came back. She stared at the bloody fabric for a few moments, and then nodded approvingly.

"Acanthus," Levana said. "You have successfully given us payment. Payment to ask us if you will be able to go back to the Underworld."

I blinked as I watched Levana, before saying, "That's right."

The seer stared at me before she spoke again.

"It is impossible to open the entranceway to Hell. Thana has been sent to the Abyss, so going back isn't an option," Levana stated matter-of-factly.

Morana nodded at her sibling's words.

"Levana is right," Morana said. "Thana is trapped now, so there is no way to go to the Abyss."

I watched the Seer Sisters as they spoke. I glared at them. I knew they were lying.

There was always a way. A way to get into Hell.

We were right near the Inferno River, so I knew that they weren't telling the truth.

Maybe I needed to remind them that I wasn't afraid of them. Maybe I needed to remind them that they could end up as food.

Food for a Minotaur.

If they didn't tell me the truth, then I could just give them to the Minotaur.

"Tell the truth, Seer Sisters," I said as I seethed, exhaling through my teeth. "If you don't, I'm dragging you both out of this swamp."

Levana blinked, startled by the ferocity in my tone. She inhaled quickly, but didn't speak as I watched her.

"Tell the truth," I growled.

Levana and Morana both froze, unable to move as I looked at them nastily.

I exhaled as I glared, and when they didn't answer, I clenched my hands into fists. I took a few steps forward, but that was when I saw Levana and Morana shake their heads.

They both spoke simultaneously.

"THERE ARE WAYS TO GET INTO HELL!" Levana and Morana screamed as I advanced.

I stopped, raising an eyebrow.

"What is it?" I asked.

"You must find the Utopian Sword," Levana told me quickly. "You must find the Utopian Sword and kill a creature or Being that has pure qualities. Then the entranceway to Hell will open. Their blood will get you into the Underworld. The Sword is hidden in the depths of a body of water in the Ethereal City. The weapon is broken, but can be mended again if you find the other portion of it. You must find the other half, Acanthus."

Morana nodded rapidly.

"Levana is telling the truth, Acanthus," she said, her voice trembling slightly.

"Who has the other half?" I asked.

"Chrysanthe does," Levana said. "Viro had it first, then the Oracle, and now it has been passed onto Chrysanthe."

I ground my teeth as I stood on the mushy ground, listening to their words. I took a few steps backward, nodding.

"Thank you," I said, the venom in my tone obsolete.

Levana spoke again.

"Acanthus, Chrysanthe is going to try to destroy you," she stated. "You, and the Minotaur that you brought with you from Hell. She is going to go to the Aerial Alpines soon, to try to find a Fire Ruby to help Phoenix. Chrysanthe is going to kill you and the Minotaur, if you're not careful."

"How do I find her?"

"You must steal the Aureate Doe from the Celestial Being known as Cyra. The deer is extremely valuable. If you capture the creature, then there is no way that Chrysanthe will succeed in her quest. Cyra will want the Doe back more than anything else in the universe. In order to stop Chrysanthe, you must first steal the Aureate Doe, and then capture Phoenix. Last, you must find the Utopian Sword."

Steal the Aureate Doe, capture Phoenix, and then find the Utopian Sword.

I soaked in Levana's words, but then seethed. I twisted around, walking away from the Seer Sisters.

Of course, Chrysanthe was going to try to destroy me, stop me and the Minotaur. Of course, she was going to try to rid the Realms of the Damned.

I knew then that I needed to stop her. I knew that from the moment she sent Thana back to the Abyss. I could stop her. Stop her and be reunited with Thana.

Thana. Thana. *Thana.*

Just the way she was treated, it made me livid.

My fake wings came out of my back as I got angry, thinking about how Thana was stabbed, killed and sent back into the Underworld. But then I felt a menacing smile on my face.

Blood was the way to open the Inferno River. Blood from someone pure. Someone pure, killed with the Utopian Sword.

Now, I needed to find the weapon...end a Being's existence...

The smile was still on my face as I flew away from the swamp.

I knew exactly whose blood I needed as I went up into the sky. Whose blood would open the Underworld again, who I needed to end.

Chrysanthe.

13

Chrysanthe

Celio's arms relaxed as his feet landed on the ground of the World Beyond. His wings flapped in front of him, and I could feel the rush of air as he steadied himself.

The sensation of it brushing my cheeks made me smile. It tickled my skin, and the feathers from Celio's wings did the same thing.

A laugh made its way through my throat, and Celio looked at me, grinning.

He leaned over, kissing my cheek.

"We're back," he said, his voice shaking slightly as he laughed.

I gazed at my surroundings.

Celio was right.

We were right in front of the Divine Castle. We were on the clouds that were a part of the Heavens.

Celio relaxed his grip on my body, and I slowly put my feet on the ground.

I smiled at my love once I was standing. He just grinned again.

Celio just gazed into my eyes, but then he shifted his focus to behind me.

"Someone's here to see you," he said, a chuckle in his voice.

I twisted my body around only to hear an affectionate nicker, and then a snort. I smiled as I saw Maximus right in front of the

Divine Castle. I walked over to the stallion, who nickered again as I ran my palm over his snout.

"You're a good horse," I told him as he pushed his head into my abdomen.

I laughed.

Maximus really was a great steed. The Winged Horse had done an amazing job when he brought me up to the Afterworld, and when Celio needed him. He was a great equine.

I was still petting the Winged Horse when I saw Nevaeh come to my side out of my peripheral vision. I brought my eyes to her.

"Maximus is so well-behaved," I commented.

"Yes, he is," Nevaeh said, nodding. "I knew he would be good for you."

My forehead scrunched together as I processed the words.

"You sent Maximus to me?"

Nevaeh nodded.

"Yes, Chrysanthe. We did. We got him from Sybella, that was how he got sent to you."

"We?" I asked.

"Beacon and I," Nevaeh clarified. "We both knew that you would need the Winged Horse to complete your tasks. We also knew that you needed a Unicorn for your last journey. To get rid of the evil, and send Thana back to Hell."

I froze, staring at her face.

"You… you helped Serenity? You helped the Floating Soul?"

Nevaeh nodded again.

"Yes. We got the horses for Serenity, and then for the both of you."

I saw Beacon come to my other side.

"Chrysanthe, we gave Serenity both horses," he told me. "We were watching over you and Celio to make sure you were both safe."

Beacon and Nevaeh were always there, watching over us.

I smiled. "Thank you for doing that," I said.

Nevaeh just smiled back at me. "You're welcome, Chrysanthe."

A grin was still on my face when I blinked.

Serenity.

Serenity was here, in the Afterworld. My father, Viro, had sent her to Heaven for helping Celio and I. She was now here. Which meant that Celio and I could see her again. We could visit Serenity.

Nevaeh saw me as my facial expression turned, as I was thinking. As if she could read my mind, Nevaeh said, "You both can see Serenity whenever you like. Just don't forget what your task is in the morning."

"Maximus will be outside early, right?" I asked.

She nodded.

"I'll wake up as early as I can, then," I said.

My eyes went back to the Winged Horse as he snorted.

I petted him gently, running my fingers through his black mane. "Are you going to be a good equine?" I asked him softly. "Are you?"

Maximus pushed his head into my chest, almost in response to what I had just asked.

I laughed, while Beacon and Nevaeh both chuckled. I looked behind me and saw Celio grinning. Then I felt a nudge on my arm, and turned around to see Nevaeh gazing into the distance.

A smile was on her face.

I glanced at her before following her line of sight. Then I saw her.

Serenity. The former Floating Soul.

Her body was clothed in a vibrant red dress, while her eyes lit up as she saw me. Her long brown hair went past her shoulders, while her brown eyes and peach-colored skin were radiant.

Serenity appeared healthy and happy as I walked toward her.

"Chrysanthe? Celio?" she asked as she saw both of us. "You're here."

I could tell that she was happy, as well as confused.

"What...? What?" she stammered. "What are you doing here, in the Afterworld?"

"There is a new threat to the Ethereal City, as well as the Heavens," I told her.

Serenity squinted as she thought. "You are here to get rid of the Minotaur and Acanthus, aren't you?"

I nodded. "Exactly," I said.

"Well, I can help you again, if you want," she stated. "I did help you on your last journey. I can do so again."

I looked at Celio, who had come up beside me.

"It always helps to have guidance," he said, grinning at Serenity.

I nodded at Celio's words. "Yes, help is always great," I said.

Serenity smiled. "Alright, I'll help you defeat the threat. You both will never be alone."

I exchanged a glance with Celio.

We were ready.

Ready to defeat the threat that was Acanthus and the Minotaur.

14

Acanthus

y feet landed in the dirt right as my wings flew out, keeping me steady.

I looked at my surroundings.

There were no Beings in the area, so I quickly ducked inside a nearby cave.

My skin crawled as I immediately turned into myself.

I'd morphed into an Archangel as I flew away from the Seer Sisters, but now, I had to change back into my Being self.

The Minotaur only recognized me when I was myself, or when I shifted into a Goblin.

The Goblin was how I'd got out of Hell once Thana had sliced through the Underworld with the Empyrean Blade.

I'd brought the Minotaur to the Ethereal City. All while I was looking like a Goblin. In order to blend in in the Ethereal City, I disguised myself first as an Archangel, then whoever was near me.

A guttural, feral sound erupted from the inside of the cave as I advanced, and I inhaled slowly at the noise.

Careful of where I was going so I wouldn't step on the bones of dead Beings, I saw the outline of the Minotaur.

He was staring right at me; his eyes were blood red. It took a few moments for him to recognize me, but when he did, he snorted.

The bull-like creature turned his back, uninterested once he recognized me.

I watched him carefully, knowing the Minotaur was unpredictable. I'd controlled him when I was in the Abyss, but he had been chained up.

Now, he was free of any restraints. It was unnerving, but the Minotaur hadn't attacked me yet.

I always had to watch him, though.

I slowly walked into the cave, hearing the crunching of bones from the inside. I knew the Minotaur was well-fed.

The bones of the deceased were everywhere in the cave, proof that he had been eating. But since all the skeletal remains were in here, the creature was staying in the cave.

He hadn't come out of it since I'd been in the Ethereal City, looking through Viro and Thera's belongings.

The Minotaur hadn't moved, but he had found a way to lure unsuspecting Beings to their death. He was able to hunt.

A grunt made its way to my ears, and I peered into the darkness of the cave. The blood-red eyes shone through the blackness, before I saw the rest of his muscles, his black fur, his horns that were as sharp as daggers.

He walked up to me on two feet, sniffing and soaking up the smells that were all around me. He exhaled roughly, and I relaxed, knowing he wouldn't attack me. Not today anyway.

He wasn't dangerous to me, but he was to the Beings in the Ethereal City and the Afterworld. Every other Being would be terrified of the Minotaur.

Every Being, except me.

15

Chrysanthe

I yawned as I walked back to the bedroom in the Divine Castle. It had been a long day. First, I had met Hali, then I'd seen Serenity again…

There were a lot of tasks to do too, like find the Fire Ruby, see Phoenix, slay the Minotaur… And that wasn't even the end of the tasks I was required to do.

I shook my head, coming back to the present.

There were just a lot of tasks that I had. But the good thing was that I wasn't going to be alone. There were Beings who would help.

That made me feel better.

Another yawn took over me; I then went to the closet and found another set of clothing to sleep in.

I changed before collapsing into the bed. I was so tired and had had a full morning, as well as night. I sighed, knowing the quest I was going to start tomorrow was going to be even more hectic. More hectic than the journey I'd been on before, when I protected the Realms from Thana.

But I was ready. Ready to get rid of the threat.

I inhaled deeply as I snuggled down in the bedsheets.

I fell asleep immediately.

The room was ink-black as I opened my eyes, my mouth wide in a yawn as I sat up in bed.

I threw my arms out, stretching, but that was when I paused.

This morning, I would be flying to the Aerial Alpines with Maximus to find the Fire Ruby.

I bit my lip anxiously.

I'd never been there, but the thought of all the Beings entered my mind. They would be with me, would help if I needed it. Plus, I knew it was on me to save them.

I exhaled. I felt a lot better knowing they would be by my side and would assist me.

I threw my arms out, loosening my muscles before I threw the sheets back, getting up from the bed. I looked around in the darkness, trying to see, but I couldn't view anything in front of me.

I knew what to do then.

Since I could control nature, take command of the weather, and mend wildlife injuries, I could easily bring some light into the room.

I brought my middle finger and thumb together, which created a spark of flames that erupted in my left palm.

Carefully, I looked around the room, before I found a jar right beside the bed to put the fire in. I brought my hand to the container, transferring the orange flames to it slowly before I put my fingers together again.

The fire in my hand abruptly disappeared.

But now I could see all around me, throughout the room.

I quickly cleaned up, making the bed under the dim lighting that illuminated throughout the space. I looked around the area once I was done, and then went to the closet once more. I found a dress, before I quickly changed. I was over by the mirror that was on the wall when I heard a light knock on the door.

"Chrysanthe," I heard Celio's soft voice on the other end. "Chrysanthe, may I come in?"

I smiled as I went over to gently open the ornate entranceway. Celio was standing there, studying my gaze.

I advanced toward him, kissing his cheek.

"Yes," I breathed, the grin still on my lips.

Celio gazed around the bedroom. "You already figured out how to bring light in," he said softly, and then brought his attention back to me. "Are you ready to go? Maximus will be outside soon," he said.

I nodded at my love. "Yes, I'm ready to go. Let me just get rid of the firelight."

I walked over to the jar, extending my hand out, opening it to extinguish the flames. I knew where I was going, since there was a little bit of light in the hallway. I could easily see where I was. I then advanced over to Celio's side.

"Remember, I'll be with you the entire journey," he said.

I nodded, and leaned forward to kiss him.

"I love you," I told him, and he smiled.

I took a quick look behind me, inspecting the bedroom, making sure it was tidy.

I walked out into the hallway, closing the ornate door behind me.

Celio and I both advanced throughout the Divine Castle. It was when we reached the entrance that I heard a whinny.

I smiled as the sound reached my ears. I glanced at Celio, who was laughing. He opened the door, and a chuckle was in my throat as I saw the Winged Horse.

Maximus snorted, throwing his wings up as he watched me.

I turned to Celio, who kissed me.

"I'll be with you," he murmured into my lips. "I'll be right behind you."

I broke away from him, peering into his eyes, and then watched the Winged Horse that was in front of me.

"Okay," I said as I exhaled, making my way over to the black stallion.

Maximus nickered as I came close, sniffing my hand. I ran my extremities over his muzzle and his mane. The equine bowed low, sticking one leg out, while he bent the other.

I grinned as I got on Maximus, looking over at Celio as I grasped the Winged Horse's mane.

Celio had come right beside Maximus; he nodded at me.

I clicked my tongue at the Winged Horse, and then Maximus snorted. I held on tight as the steed whinnied, rearing up on his hind legs, and threw his wings out toward the sky. Once he was on all four hooves, he started galloping.

I gripped his mane tighter as he picked up speed, and within moments he was airborne.

Airborne and headed to the Aerial Alpines.

16

Wind blew through my hair as Maximus flew away from the Afterworld, climbing higher and higher into the sky with each flap of his wings.

They brushed against my cheeks as the Winged Horse navigated through the clouds, and I smiled at the sensation.

A few moments later, he made his way above the masses of water particles that were in the air.

I took a deep breath, glancing down, noticing just how far up in the sky we were. The sunlight began to stream through the atmosphere as it began to rise, and my heart was pounding as I realized how high up Maximus had taken me.

I gripped the stallion's mane as a result, holding it tightly.

He was flying through the atmosphere for a while.

Maximus snorted as he started to descend. He whinnied as he broke away from the clouds, and that was when I saw the gargantuan mountain range below me.

Part of the peaks were so large that they went right into the atmosphere, straight through the clouds.

The Aerial Alpines.

The equine's wings flapped as we approached the rocky terrain, and he threw them behind his body as he slowed down.

Maximus partly reared up in the air as he went toward the ground. He then hit the mountainous terrain with his back hooves.

I held on tight as his front hooves descended. He galloped for a few moments before slowing down and stopping.

His wings were high in the air as he did so, flapping as he slowed down.

It was after that that he halted completely.

I smiled as I ran my hands over his mane, praising him, before I looked around at my surroundings.

The Aerial Alpines were named correctly; I could see that not just one, but all of the mountaintops reached into the sky.

I just sat on Maximus' back, marveling at the rocky surroundings before I blinked, coming back to myself.

The Aerial Alpines were just so huge…

A flapping sound resounded in my ears as I peered around; I turned and smiled.

Celio grinned as he landed, and Maximus nickered softly when he saw the Archangel.

I climbed off the Winged Horse and walked over to Celio, wrapping my arms around him.

"Hello, again," he said as I looked in his eyes.

I kissed his cheek. "Hi," I responded.

He turned his attention to the Aerial Alpines. He then looked back at me, extending his hand out to hold mine.

"Alright, Chrysanthe," he said. "Let's go find the Aureate Doe."

17

Acanthus

teal the Aureate Doe, capture Phoenix, and find the Utopian Sword. The thoughts circulated inside my mind as I leaned against the side of the cave. They were on repeat in my head.

I blinked, coming back to the present as I heard a grunt and a rough exhale; the Minotaur walked toward me from the depths of the darkness.

He looked into my eyes; the bull-creature stared for several moments before he brought his attention to the forest outside.

The Minotaur was hungry.

Even though he had had food in the form of other Beings, he still needed more.

The Minotaur glanced at me again, before retreating into the blackness of the cave.

I could hear him stepping on bones with his hooves, crunching them. He was just going to have to wait until nightfall to go hunting. That way, no Being would be able to see him.

The Minotaur would blend into the night, into the darkness. He would be able to feed then.

I thought about that for a moment, about the bull-like creature feeding at night, when I suddenly had another thought come across my brain.

The creature was always needing food, and I did, at one point, have to capture Phoenix.

Phoenix, the oldest Celestial Being in existence.

Maybe...Maybe... I could feed Phoenix to the Minotaur. Phoenix, or the Aureate Doe.

A sick smile erupted on my face, and I looked into the darkness again, seeing only the Minotaur's red eyes.

That was what I was going to do; I was going to find Phoenix and the Aureate Doe, and bring them to the monster that hid in the cave.

The only thing was that I had to find the Aureate Doe before I could find the shapeshifting Being.

I had to steal the Doe from Cyra, from the Aerial Alpines. I knew that was where she was, deep in the mountains. I also knew that that was where Chrysanthe was as well.

I had to stop Chrysanthe.

Stop Chrysanthe from destroying me.

18

Chrysanthe

Celio and I were holding hands and walking through the rocky trails when we both heard a voice.

We turned at the same moment, and then paused as we saw a beautiful Celestial Being inside an opening in the surroundings.

She was wearing a very vibrant yellow dress, while her golden hair blew in the breeze. She wore jewelry the same color as her mane. She had a shimmering doe tattoo on her wrist that was also the same hue as her hair.

"Hello," she said once we saw her. "Hello, Chrysanthe. Hello, Celio," the Being said, taking us both off guard. "I'm Cyra."

I blinked and looked at Celio, who had the same bewildered expression on his face.

"Sybella has told me about you both," Cyra said, watching both of our faces. "That's how I know."

Celio nodded, while I just stood there.

"The Oracle told me you need to find the Fire Ruby to give to Phoenix," she said, to which I nodded.

"Yes. Yes, that is correct," I said.

Cyra looked at Celio and I for a few moments, before she spoke.

"I left the Fire Ruby with the Aureate Doe. She guards the gold and jewels that belong to me. You're going to have to find her. Once you do, you will be able to get what you need."

"Is there anything else we need to do to get the Ruby?"

Cyra nodded before she spoke. "Chrysanthe, you must bring a piece of my jewelry with you. I'll give you one of my necklaces."

She removed the object, and she placed it around my neck.

I smiled at Cyra as it fell to the base of my throat.

"Now, Chrysanthe, you will have to put this around the Doe's neck, and you will find the Fire Ruby. It is red-orange, and will help Phoenix greatly."

I nodded. "How do we find the Aureate Doe?"

As I said that a whinny was heard in the distance.

Cyra smiled. "The Winged Horse can certainly assist you," she said.

I turned around, only to see the stallion land on the rough terrain. I grinned.

Maximus was going to bring me to the Aureate Doe.

I twisted back toward Cyra.

"If you need me, I'll be here," she said. Then she watched Celio and I. "Good luck. to the both of you. Also, Chrysanthe, here is a bag to put the Fire Ruby in once you find it."

She gave me a medium-sized crossbody bag, and then smiled.

"Good luck," Cyra repeated as she looked at Celio and I.

I spotted the Aureate Doe as Maximus was flying over the mountains.

The deer was shimmering, exactly like Cyra's tattoo. She was sparkling in the sunlight, glittering as I pulled gently on the Winged Horse's mane.

The stallion whinnied as he descended; within moments he hit the ground with his back hooves, rearing before throwing his wings out. He immediately slowed down as I looked at the golden deer that was nearby, and slowly dismounted as Maximus nickered.

I heard Celio land right behind me; I turned to see him grin.

Celio walked toward me, and I brought my attention back to the Aureate Doe, who was staring at us with chocolate brown eyes. She also had a beautiful sparkling fur coat. When the sunlight hit her body, she was stunning.

The Doe was in an open area of the rocky terrain, tucked in the side of the mountain. She slowly walked up to me as I advanced toward her, and then I remembered the necklace.

The deer cautiously sniffed my hand before I slowly removed the gold jewelry Cyra had given me.

I placed it around the Doe's neck, to which she walked forward more, letting me pet her and rub her ears. She seemed entirely relaxed, nudging me for more attention.

Celio chuckled as he saw me with the Doe, and it was a few moments later that I noticed the pile of gold and jewels which were tucked away, the items the deer was protecting.

I stroked the deer's head one last time before I made my way over to the objects. It didn't take long to find the Fire Ruby; its red-orange color made it easy to spot. I ran my thumb over the Ruby as I held it in my palm.

My eyes locked with Celio's as he stood outside.

The Aureate Doe was sniffing him warily, but Celio's gaze was on me.

I felt my expression turn into a happy one as I looked at my love.

I had found the Fire Ruby that would help Phoenix.

Now, I just had to complete the next task.

19

Acanthus

A rough exhale exited my lungs as I continued to lean against the cave wall, my thoughts moving around in my head quickly. I turned toward the darkness of the tunnel, hearing the Minotaur breathe, when I abruptly heard a flapping sound. I brought my eyes to the outside, where the surroundings were bright and sunny, only to see a barn owl perched on a tree branch close by.

My brows scrunched together, my eyes narrowing.

I stared at the creature, trying to figure out why the bird was there, when I growled.

The barn owl wasn't just any animal as I saw it swivel its head around, watching me intently.

I knew who it *really* was then.

It was Sybella.

It was Sybella, Chrysanthe's former mentor.

The former mentor who also drowned Thana in the Inferno River as a baby.

Thana was then left in Hell. She'd ruled the Abyss ever since.

My teeth ground together as I seethed, glaring at Sybella. The rumble was still in my throat as I stared at her, disgusted.

She clacked her beak together.

My eyes were slits; I couldn't believe that the Oracle had found not only me, but the Minotaur as well. Air scraped through my lungs as my feet suddenly hit a rock.

I hadn't realized that I had taken a few steps forward. I leaned over, grabbing the object. I glanced at the barn owl for only a moment or two before I saw her eyes widen.

Sybella flew off the tree branch at the exact moment I threw the rock toward her with all my strength. The object missed her by inches, and an animalistic screech erupted from the shapeshifter as she disappeared into the sky.

Fury pulsed through me, soaking my bloodstream as I watched the Oracle fly away.

I heard a snort right beside me, and I turned to see the Minotaur looking straight ahead, following where the owl had taken off. I watched him for a moment, and that was when I saw him lick his muzzle.

If the Oracle, Sybella, returned, she would be food for the Minotaur.

I stayed in the cave for a while; the Minotaur had walked deep within the darkness. The sun set and the light disappeared.

My eyes were glued to the black sky. I was staring into space as I heard the creature again.

He came to the entrance, looked at me, and snorted. Then he walked out into the woods, a heavy exhale exiting his lungs. Since he was under the cover of darkness, the Minotaur could now go hunt.

I looked over at him, watching, before I just followed the creature out into the forest.

20

I followed the Minotaur under the cover of the night, walking beside him as his rough breathing filled my ears. I glanced at him at the same moment that his eyes locked with mine.

His red ones burned as I watched him. The creature twisted around and took off in the direction of the Ethereal City.

I was right behind the Minotaur as we made it out of the woods, air soaring through my teeth as I did so.

I stopped where I was as I reached the edge of the forest. Right in front of the Ethereal City. I saw the Minotaur walk forward, as I stayed where I was.

I knew I needed to morph, so that no Being would recognize me. I glanced up at the moon which illuminated the ink-black night, and started to shift.

I felt my skin crawl for a few moments, before I shrank.

Suddenly, I had feathers, and black wings. I had shifted into a crow.

I clacked my beak as I flew off, into the Ethereal City; I wanted to go back to Viro and Thera's old bedchamber.

I wanted to see if there was anything else I could steal from them.

Hopefully, I would find something. Something of value I could take with me when I had to do my first task.

My first task of stealing the Aureate Doe.

I knew that the Doe was extremely valuable, but also, the deer was protecting jewels and objects that were rare and valuable as well.

The Aureate Doe was named the Aureate because she was golden, because of the Being named Cyra. She could turn anything she touched into gold. Cyra harnessed the sun's power and light to turn anything. Cyra had renamed it, and then used the animal to protect her valuable items.

In order to get close to the Aureate Doe, I would have to have an object that was significant enough to distract the deer.

Distract her, and then steal her.

I flew through the open window to Viro and Thera's old bedchamber yet again. As soon as I did, I immediately shifted back into myself.

I peered around the now dark room, looking in the blackness that surrounded me.

That was when I saw it, the object I needed.

A box of powder. Not just any powder though, this was from Phoenix.

It was a mixture of his ashes, from when he morphed. Every time he shifted, he would lose some of his power. There was power in these ashes. They could be used for good, or evil.

I snarled, a sick smile erupting over my face.

Now, I knew exactly what to do, and exactly how to trap both the Aureate Doe and Phoenix.

All I needed to do now was find them.

21

Chrysanthe

Sunlight bounced off the Fire Ruby as it sparkled in the brightness. Like the name suggested, it was a red-orange color, resembling a blaze.

I held it in the air for a few more moments before putting it into the crossbody bag that Cyra had given me.

I had completed the first task, to find the gemstone.

Now, I had to bring the Fire Ruby to Phoenix, the oldest Celestial Being in existence.

My eyes turned to the Aerial Alpines once the stone was secure in my bag, and I just was standing on the rocky ground, looking at the surroundings, when I saw a shadow overhead, heard a rustling of wings.

It was Maximus, the black Winged Horse. He had come to bring me to the Ethereal City, where Phoenix lived.

I smiled as I saw Maximus bow, enabling me to climb onto the stallion's back.

I took a fistful of his mane, holding on tight before he extended his wings.

Within moments, he was flying.

Task one was done.

Now, I had to complete task number two, giving the Fire Ruby to Phoenix.

Acanthus

I seethed as my muscles tensed; I opened and closed my hands, making fists as my teeth ground against each other.

I was partly angry, and then partly expecting what I needed to do next.

Partly upset, but partly excited.

Now I had the ability to ruin Chrysanthe's existence.

I could destroy everything she held dear, including her parents.

But, right now, I had to find the Aureate Doe and Phoenix.

The Aureate Doe was in the Aerial Alpines, while I would need to capture Phoenix in the Ethereal City and overpower him, since I now had his ashes.

I had the ability to take control over the oldest Celestial Being in existence, and, eventually, destroy him.

A maniacal smile erupted on my face as I just thought about the idea.

This was going to be fun. This was going to be incredibly fun.

23

Chrysanthe

Maximus' body turned as we navigated through the clouds, as I clung to his mane.

I held on tight as his wings flapped, and could feel him shift once more as he descended toward the Ethereal City.

My heart pounded as the wind kissed my cheeks, and it was after a few moments that the Winged Horse threw out his feathered appendages. He slowed down before his back hooves hit the ground of the City.

Maximus snorted as he trotted for a bit, before he came to a complete stop.

He nickered affectionately as I pet his ink black fur.

"You're a great horse, Maximus. You're so good."

I smiled as I pet him for one more time before dismounting.

Celio arrived just a little while later.

He smiled when he saw me, before walking forward and kissing my lips.

"Hi, Chrysanthe," he said softly, in a way that made my body feel like it was melting.

"Hi, Celio," I responded, watching his eyes.

I wrapped my arms around him, and then let him go, looking at my surroundings.

The warmth that had enveloped my system from seeing my love quickly evaporated.

The Ethereal City was mostly vacant, among the twilight dusk.

It seemed like Celio and I were the only ones here.

I did notice some other Beings, but there was just a handful of them.

Everyone else seemed to have vanished, and the Beings on the grounds appeared incredibly unnerved, terrified.

I ground my teeth thinking about Acanthus and the Minotaur.

All the Celestial Beings were absolutely, positively petrified.

I hadn't noticed that my body had stiffened until I felt Celio's hand on my shoulder.

A growl ripped through my teeth as I stared at the empty streets.

This was terrible.

I continued to seethe as my eyes hit a dark shadowy area that appeared incredibly eerie.

I began walking over there, when I felt a brush on my arm.

I turned my attention to Celio, before he just followed me.

I stopped right in my tracks once I was able to see what was underneath the dark space.

I gasped, and then it was Celio's turn to seethe.

The frightening shadowy area was filled with bones.

Bones of the dead.

I inhaled quickly once more, while Celio clenched his hands into fists.

I couldn't believe it.

It almost made me sick to my stomach.

My temples became sweaty as I started to panic, but then I heard an animalistic, piercing shriek.

Both Celio and I whipped our heads around, looking up at the sky, only to see a barn owl fly toward us.

My muscles relaxed as I saw the owl, knowing by the coloring and the mannerisms that it was Sybella.

But the way that she had shrieked… That wasn't like her.

It wasn't like Sybella to sound alarmed, even in her animal form.

I glanced over at Celio, who, like me, abruptly felt worried.

We watched as Sybella flew toward the ground, before a white light engulfed her.

Quickly, the owl body that she had been in disappeared, and Sybella landed in the form of her Being self.

Both Celio and I were on alert as we saw her eyes widen, fear drenching her.

Sybella was breathing rapidly, before she gathered herself together as much as possible.

Then she spoke.

"Chrysanthe," she said in between breaths.

She looked me dead in the eyes.

"Chrysanthe, the Minotaur is on the loose right now."

As if he understood what Sybella was saying, Maximus snorted, rearing up, and then extended his wings and galloped. Within moments, he was airborne.

My heart was smashing my ribs in horror, and I looked at Celio, who had a similar expression on his face.

I gulped, glancing at Sybella, before I saw her eyes get even bigger, if that was even possible.

My breathing became rapid, and I heard a deep, formidable, feral snort, followed by an intimidating grunt.

Right behind me.

24

I turned around, my insides making me feel like I was in the middle of a bonfire.

My eyes were wide as I twisted around to see what was behind me, only to see a gigantic black bull like creature with piercing, red, angry eyes.

It moved its lip up in a snarl, and that was when I realized that the beast that I had come face to face with was the Minotaur.

The Minotaur.

The Minotaur.

It was Thana's Beast staring at me, angrily, hungrily.

The terrifying creature continued to stare before it licked its lips as its red eyes blazed.

I was so stunned, I couldn't move. But then the sound of flapping hit my ears.

A furious rumbling noise erupted through the air, almost like a roar, and I was taken aback as I saw Maximus' wings extend out from behind the Minotaur.

The Winged Horse roared as he reared up on his hind legs that had just hit the ground, and smacked the massive black creature squarely in the chest with his front hooves.

My mouth opened in shock, my jaw feeling like it had hit the floor as I saw Thana's gigantic monster hit the ground.

A sharp, quick, unmistakable groan escaped the Minotaur as it fell.

I glanced over at Maximus, only to see his ears flat against his head, his teeth showing as the Minotaur got up, a growl ripping through the creature's throat.

But Maximus stood his ground and even kicked at the Beast.

Maximus bit the Minotaur as it came closer to him, and the Winged Horse once again reared, flapping his feathered appendages roughly.

This caused the Minotaur to snarl, showing his teeth, before Maximus finally ripped out some of the creature's fur, flinging the Minotaur to the ground as Maximus became airborne.

The Minotaur slammed into the ground of the Ethereal City, becoming unconscious as Maximus' hooves hit the floor.

It was once the Minotaur was knocked out that Maximus came right up to me, whinnying affectionately, shoving his head into my stomach. He nickered, and I smiled as I pet him, stroking his mane and his ears.

"Thank you," I told the Winged Horse as he rubbed his head into my abdomen. "Thank you so much."

I glanced over at Sybella, whose eyes were so wide that they could have fallen out of her head.

She stared at the now knocked out Minotaur, and looked at me, dumbfounded.

The Winged Horse nickered again, and another grin took over my face, before he began rubbing his head into Sybella's shoulder.

It was almost as if Maximus could sense the Oracle's uneasy behavior, sense that she was anxious.

She petted him, and a few moments later, he turned back toward me.

I rubbed his neck calmly, feeling relaxed as I did so.

Maximus had protected me.

Protected me from the Minotaur.

25

Acanthus

I looked down as I flew over the Aerial Alpines, my hawk eyes immediately finding the Aureate Doe.

I had shifted into the body of the black creature, and was drifting among the clouds before I spotted the glittering animal around the rocky landscape.

I saw her, and that was when my eyes turned into slits.

I just needed to steal her, and that was how I was going to get to Chrysanthe...

I flew downward, toward the mountainous area, and I threw my body forward so I could land. I did so, and that was when I abruptly shivered, turning back into my Being self.

My lip quivered in disgust as I glimpsed at the Doe, who was hiding in the shadowy portion underneath the rocky landscape.

She was so sickeningly pure, so perfect, so golden... It was vile.

To the point where I had to hold back the bile that I felt rising in my throat.

I glared as I watched her, and then she turned and saw me.

She snorted anxiously, automatically backing up into a corner.

I walked toward the Doe, and I saw, out of the corner of my eye, my hands turning into fists, my vine and thorn Fate Tattoos snaking around and choking my arms.

I saw the Doe's eyes widen in fear as I grinned in a sinister way, and I noticed that I still had the Enchanted Powder with me. I had brought it from the Ethereal City, and had had it in my talons as I had flown here, to the Aerial Alpines.

The Powder was in my clenched fist.

I smiled as I saw the Aureate Doe begin to shake in a corner, covered by the shadows.

I seethed, ready to take the golden creature, when I quickly realized that something wasn't right.

I blinked rapidly, only to notice what was wrong.

The Fire Ruby, the most important gemstone in existence, the one stone that Phoenix needed, was gone.

I growled deeply, but that just scared the Aureate Doe more.

I quickly shifted into a crow, flying away to where Cyra was, gritting my teeth.

I still had the Enchanted Powder as I shifted once more, this time into the body of a gigantic python.

I grabbed hold of the Powder with my mouth, slithering out from behind the rock, and saw Cyra.

She saw me the moment I came out from behind the rock, blinking rapidly.

I could see in her face that she was ready to turn me into gold, ready to incapacitate me, when she caught sight of the Enchanted Powder in my mouth. Her eyes widened.

It would help or harm not only Phoenix but also any other Celestial Being that was near the Powder.

The Powder could destroy any Being, and also paralyze them so they couldn't use their powers.

Cyra glared at me, her eyes slits, ready to turn me into a frozen, gold statue, when I slithered up to her in my python form at lightning speed.

I crushed the box of Enchanted Powder with my teeth, sending the mixture airborne.

It settled on Cyra, immediately paralyzing her, rendering her immobile.

All she could do was move her eyes and make a throaty noise that was a mixture of a sob and a scream.

I shifted back into my Being form, glaring at her while she watched me, looking terrified. I smiled, enjoying the way that I was scaring Cyra.

I laughed cruelly, before I shapeshifted into a crow, taking off and flying to where the Aureate Doe was.

Then I shifted back into myself, throwing the remaining Enchanted Powder over the Doe, knocking her out immediately.

I morphed once more, this time into a black hawk, and grasped the unconscious golden creature with my talons.

I flew off, as Cyra let out a muffled scream.

The Aureate Doe had been taken from her.

26

I flew back to the Ethereal City and was disguised as the black hawk with the Aureate Doe in my talons.

When I reached the cave in the forest, I dumped the golden creature on the ground, changing back into myself quickly.

My body quivered, and it was once I was in my Being form that I walked over to the Doe, inspecting her to make sure she was unconscious.

She was, but she was still breathing.

My lips quivered as I sneered.

The Aureate Doe would be food for the Minotaur.

I smiled darkly before I extended my tattooed arms out, grasping the Aureate Doe by her hind legs and dragging her to the mouth of the cave.

Although, I paused as I entered the dark area.

Wait a moment, I thought as I turned my head around, looking in the blackness.

I couldn't hear the Minotaur at all.

The feral, guttural sounds, the unmistakable snort...

I couldn't hear anything.

I realized the creature wasn't in the cave, and I clenched my hands into fists.

My demeanor instantly changed, when I suddenly heard grunting behind me.

I twisted around to see the Minotaur, and that was when I sucked in a breath.

The Beast was battered, bruised, and had several scrapes on his hide. He was still able to walk, though.

He just looked at me before walking into the cave, another grunt escaping him.

My lip curled upward in disgust.

Some Being had harmed the Minotaur. Some Being, or some creature.

And whoever or whatever that was was going to pay the price. Pay the ultimate price.

Death.

27

Chrysanthe

My breathing was so quick, I thought I was going to pass out.

My heart was pumping blood so quickly, it felt like I had been running for miles.

I blinked for several moments before I shook my head, attempting to clear it.

I just couldn't believe this.

I had almost been attacked by my sister's Minotaur.

Her Minotaur.

I sniffled as I thought about what could've happened to me, and that was when I felt arms wrap around my body.

My head hung low as tears started to flow down my cheeks, and I turned my head and buried it into Celio's shoulder, sobbing into his clothing.

His hand stroked my back as my tears soaked his shirt, and I brought my hands up from my sides. I hugged him tightly.

I squeezed his body as hard as I could, trying to get rid of the memory that had happened earlier.

But then I felt Celio's hand leave my back, and I pulled away from his shoulder to look my love in the eyes.

Celio brought his hand up to my raw cheek, grasping my jaw gently. He watched my face for a few moments before he leaned forward and kissed me.

When he pulled away, he stroked the skin under my eyes.

They felt like raw meat, but my body tingled as he touched me.

He just looked at me with his powerful gaze, and I blinked rapidly before he spoke.

"Chrysanthe," he said. "Chrysanthe, you're safe now. You have nothing to worry about. You're going to be alright."

I stared at him.

I felt like I was getting stronger, more confident, as I looked at him, his hazel eyes.

I took a deep breath, steadying myself, and that was when I felt my heartrate slow down.

I became calmer as I closed my eyes, gathering myself together once more.

Celio was right.

I was going to be okay.

I was safe now.

Sybella had brought both Celio and I to her living quarters, which appeared incredibly comfortable and relaxing.

She had a deep red carpet that engulfed the entire area, while there was a crystal ball on a table nearby.

I took another deep breath as I looked at my surroundings.

The ceiling was designed to appear like the night sky, with stars throughout the dark 'atmosphere'.

Altogether, the energy here was calm.

Calm and cozy.

The living quarters were absolutely stunning.

I turned toward Sybella.

"Thank you," I told her.

"You're welcome," she replied. "You must stay here tonight. Since the Minotaur has been knocked unconscious by Maximus, the Hell Being, Acanthus, will retaliate. Retaliate under the cover of darkness. You must stay here."

Sybella sounded stern, serious.

The tone of voice that she had was enough to make Celio and I nod immediately in agreement.

"Okay, we understand," Celio and I said simultaneously.

I nodded at Sybella's words.

"Alright," the Oracle said as she looked at the both of us.

It seemed like the Oracle had breathed a sigh of relief once we had spoken. I could see her becoming relaxed.

"Okay, then. Well, let me show you around my quarters," she said. "I'll show you where everything is so you don't get lost or confused."

Celio and I looked at each other, before turning to the Oracle.

"Alright," we said together.

Sybella turned, and Celio and I followed her.

Sybella's living quarters were massive, as well as decorated.

Red carpeting covered the entire floor, while there were celestial designs on the wall; stars and astrological symbols over the walls of her chambers.

I blinked when I saw the eclectic symbols.

I knew mortals believed in symbols, and they were attached to their birthdays.

The astrological designs had an interesting way of weaving into the mortal's culture. I knew some people trusted these symbols and designs to live their lives.

Then again, if they learned about Celestial Beings being a part of their world and culture, and how everything was true, we would be a giant part of their existence as well.

Sybella clearing her throat brought me back to the present, and I blinked before I looked at her and realized that we had gotten to the bedchamber.

The comforter and the pillows were a dark red when I took in the look of the bed, while the rest of the sheets were a lighter, golden color.

I pulled my eyes away when I heard the Oracle speak.

"I usually enjoy sleeping in the form of the barn owl," she said, nodding over to the makeshift perch in the other room. "This room is yours, if you wish. There are also couches outside if you want to sleep on those. Choose whatever you want. But for me," she opened her mouth to yawn, "I'm going to go shift and go sleep on my perch."

The Oracle then turned around before walking into the other room. A few moments later, I heard the flapping of wings.

The Oracle had shifted.

I glanced over at Celio, who smiled and kissed my cheek.

"I'll take the couch, Chrysanthe. You can take the bed."

I looked at him, at the smile that was still on his lips. I nodded at my love, and I grinned.

"Okay, Celio. Alright."

Acanthus

I ground my teeth together in anger as I stood outside in the woods, under the cover of darkness.

The sky was ink-black now that the sun had set.

I wanted to stay in the dark wooded area for a while, trying to decompress from what I saw earlier.

The Minotaur.

He had gotten battered and bruised.

Not only that, but the creature hadn't even touched the Aureate Doe.

The deer was still breathing, although she was unconscious.

I was expecting the Minotaur to feed, but apparently that wasn't going to happen.

A growl ripped through me and my face got contorted into a snarl.

But then, a thought occurred to me.

The Minotaur wouldn't feed.

The Aureate Doe wasn't going to be eaten.

But, maybe, her blood could open the entryway to Hell.

The entrance guarded by the Seer Sisters, Levana and Morana.

I paused as I continued that thought.

The Seer Sisters once told me about the Utopian Sword, and how a pure Being or creature could open the entrance.

Which meant that the Aureate Doe wouldn't be enough.

Also, Levana had told me there was a specific order to the tasks to be completed.

I scrunched my eyebrows together as I tried to think back to what Levana had told me.

The next task was... was...

I opened my eyes when I realized it, and seethed in anticipation.

The next thing I had to do was capture Phoenix.

I felt myself shrink as I morphed into the black crow, before flying to the Ethereal City.

The Ethereal City had the Elysian Manor, where the Celestial Beings lived before the Ceremony that determined their permanent home. Like Chrysanthe being the Protector of the Earth.

I wanted to curl my lip upward in disgust, but I couldn't do that since I was a crow at the moment.

Ugh, I thought.

Chrysanthe was incredibly perfect; she could do no wrong.

And it was nauseating.

My wings flapped quickly as I made my way to the Manor, where Thera and Viro's bedchamber was.

Since they were the King and Queen of all Celestials, their home, their *original* home, was in the Elysian Manor.

I landed near the front window, only to realize they all had been locked up; I was barred from entering.

I sensed my crow eyes narrowing before I flew away, aggravated.

Now I was really losing my temper.

I guessed I would have to go about capturing Phoenix another way.

I would have to do some thinking on that one.

29

I flew away from the Elysian Manor.

I landed in the Ethereal City, before I shifted back into my Being self.

I snarled in frustration as I stomped around, before I saw an area of the City that was incredibly dark and covered in shadows.

A menacing smile crept up on my lips as I walked up to the spot; I'd been staring at it for several moments.

I heard a crunch as soon as I went over.

Then another.

And another.

I scrunched my eyebrows together in confusion, looking down, before I realized the noise was the remnants of the Celestial Beings, the bones of the dead, being crushed beneath my feet.

The Minotaur's victims.

I grinned again as I looked at the ground that was surrounded by death.

An idea started to form.

I was going to poison the Ethereal City, poison the City with my Hell Tattoos.

If the Ethereal City was touched by a Being from the Underworld, a Being whose Fate Tattoos are literally filled with poison, if the City was buried in toxins, every Being who lived there would eventually die.

The Ethereal City would be destroyed.

And I was going to do exactly that.

Destroy the Ethereal City, and the Beings who lived there.

I grinned a sick grin as I scraped my arms and my Fate Tattoos with my fingernails.

The plant vines were wrapped around my upper limbs like a python with its meal.

It only took a few moments, but eventually the Fate Tattoo became real, climbing from my skin.

They snaked around everything in sight, moving incredibly fast on the grounds of the Ethereal City.

A maniacal laugh escaped from deep within my throat; I was immune to the toxins.

Plus, they were creating destruction.

Now I knew what I was going to do.

I was going to obliterate the Ethereal City, and everyone inside it.

30

Chrysanthe

I inhaled quickly as I tried to take in my surroundings, but I could feel my body quivering, my heart pulverizing my ribs, making me think that they were going to break.

I was just surrounded by darkness.

Inky blackness surrounded me as sweat began to pool in my palms, starting to dampen the back of my neck.

The bodily fluid began to soak my blond hair, and I quickly moved my mane away from my neck, attempting to get rid of the hot, sticky sensation that was engulfing the nape of it.

But that didn't work; I still felt incredibly uncomfortable.

I looked up eventually, only to see that the only light was from the moon.

It cut through the darkness like a knife, but it was after I turned away from the moon that I realized I was in deep trouble.

I was in an eerie-looking forest.

Not only that, but there was a lake in front of me, breaking up the woods.

My heart was now pulverizing my ribs as I felt my stomach begin to twist; I was on the verge of vomiting as I began walking toward the lake.

I had the sensation of uneasiness creeping up inside me as I walked toward the water, which reflected the moon.

I took a deep breath, trying to steady my heartrate, before I looked into the liquid.

I was expecting to see my reflection.

But instead, I saw half of my reflection, half of my face, while the other half was... was... Thana's.

I stood up and stared into the liquid, unable to move for several moments, before I finally pulled myself away from the eerie sight.

I started hyperventilating, and looked down at my body, only to see a crow tattoo on my chest and throat, as well as a scary-looking skull on my wrist.

A scream ripped through my chest as I realized that I had my twin's tattoos, both appearing incredibly unnerving in the moonlight.

I now had my sister's Fate Tattoos...

I inhaled sharply, waking up instantly as I was ready to scream.

It took only two moments to realize it was just a dream.

My heart was racing, and the bedsheets were soaked in sweat.

I tried to regulate my breathing, trying to calm my pounding heart, but I quickly gave up, climbing from the bed drenched in perspiration.

I went outside the bedchamber, going to where the couches were, where Celio was sleeping.

I blinked, suddenly calm.

Being with my love, even when he was asleep, was incredibly soothing.

I watched him as his diaphragm rose and fell, when I heard a flapping sound.

I turned just in time to see Sybella transform into her Being self.

Sybella caught the look of anxiety that quickly passed through my face as I turned toward the bedchamber that I'd been in, as I brought my attention to it.

Not to mention I was soaked in sweat.

"Chrysanthe?" Sybella asked, the sound of her voice making me look at her. "Chrysanthe, what happened? What's wrong?"

31

S ybella's eyes locked on mine, her face an expression of concern.

I sniffled slightly as the memory of the dream took over my brain.

"I had... had... had a dream, or really, a nightmare, that I was in a forest at night. The only light source was the moon, but when I went to a lake that was nearby, I... I saw my reflection. But I saw my reflection mixed with... with Thana's."

I paused, looking at Sybella, who didn't show much emotion at me bringing up Thana, my evil twin.

"I even saw her Fate Tattoos on my body. The crow on my chest, with one of its wings on my throat. The crow, and the disturbing-looking skull on my wrist. I had both of her Fate Tattoos, and, and, then as they appeared on my body, as soon as I realized that I had Thana's tattoos, I woke up."

I watched the Oracle, watched her face carefully, before she sighed.

It was after she sighed that she began to speak.

"Chrysanthe," she said in a calm tone, "Chrysanthe, because you were marked by Thana, you can have dreams about your twin, who is now trapped in Hell. This is also happening because the incantation I cast is wearing off. I have to say it again," Sybella stated.

The Oracle touched my arm, saying the incantation once more.

Sybella spoke again once the spell had been cast.

"The only way to truly break the tie between you and Thana permanently would be to kill the Minotaur and Acanthus."

I nodded understandingly, before turning my attention to my love, who was still fast asleep.

Celio looked so peaceful as he dozed...

I leaned forward, brushing his hair out of his face and off his forehead.

I gently touched his skin, leaning forward and kissing his cheek.

I saw Celio's eyes flutter as he woke up.

Acanthus

I watched my Fate Tattoos as they coiled around everything in sight.

The thorny vines were damaging anything and everything in its path.

The sharp tips of the plant-like tattoo were killer, since my Fate Tattoos were poisonous.

Any Being who attempted to get past them would prick their finger and would immediately bleed.

Not only that, but they would get venom in their system just from the vines.

I smiled darkly, and watched as my Fate Tattoos snaked around everything, becoming thick brambles.

It was now blocking everything in any Celestial Being's path.

So now, the Beings would either stay in the Elysian Manor, or get poisoned instantly by my Fate Tattoo that was covering everything on the grounds of the Ethereal City.

For the Beings, it would either be stay in the Elysian Manor, or die.

I sneered, knowing I had the upper hand now, and I was able to have full control.

I smiled, knowing how terrible the Beings must've felt.

I grinned a sick, twisted grin, before I quickly shivered, changing into a bat, and flew away.

The thorns and brambles meanwhile engulfed the entire outside grounds of the Ethereal City.

Celio

My eyes slowly opened to the sensation of Chrysanthe gently pushing my hair back from my forehead. The feeling of her fingers in my hair sent a warm sensation fluttering down my spine.

We smiled at each other as I locked eyes with her, and put my hand on her cheek before I kissed her.

"Good morning," I breathed, grinning at Chrysanthe.

I turned to the Oracle, who was beside her.

"Thank you, Sybella," I said. "Thank you for giving us a place to stay."

Chrysanthe looked over at Sybella, before she spoke as well.

"Yes, thank you, Sybella."

"You're welcome," the Oracle responded to the both of us. "I knew both of you had to be in a safe place, away from Acanthus. As I said before, he will retaliate."

Right after Sybella said that, there was a blood-curdling screech outside.

Immediately, I went over to the window, Chrysanthe following right behind me.

It was a Celestial Being who had pricked her finger on thorny vines, which had taken over the grounds of the Ethereal City.

Sybella joined Chrysanthe and I as the Being started to hyperventilate, but unfortunately, that just made the bleeding worse.

Blood was gushing from the wound.

And it wasn't stopping.

My forehead crinkled as I took in the scene, confusion taking over.

Why wasn't it stopping?

My muscles tightened as I looked at the Being.

I felt unnerved.

Two moments later, I turned to the Oracle.

"I need to go help her," I said immediately, and Sybella nodded understandingly.

She instantly went over to the entrance of her living quarters, opening the door quickly, and that was when I took my shirt off, revealing my Fate Tattoo.

I gave the garment to Chrysanthe, kissing her gently.

"I'll be back, I promise," I told her softly.

I turned around afterward, rolling my shoulders forward, and I could feel my Archangel wings come out of my back.

I inhaled, exhaling slowly, and then flew off toward the injured Being.

34

I flew away from the Oracle's living quarters, going toward the ground of the Ethereal City.

Now, the Being was bleeding profusely.

I landed with my wings completely wrapped around me.

The feathery appendages were massive as I went over to the Being, but one look at her told me that she was past the point of saving.

My teeth ground together in frustration and anger as she stared at me.

She appeared delirious, and that was when I looked at the vines, a closer look.

Then I squinted, remembering one bit of information about Acanthus.

His Fate Tattoos were toxic, they had venom in them.

That was why the Being was bleeding so much, and the reason she appeared to be losing her focus on my face, at which she had been staring.

I bit my lip as I watched her, holding back my emotions, but I could see her blink.

She took a breath, one final breath, and then exhaled.

When the Celestial Being exhaled, she became still.

She had passed away.

35

I gritted my teeth together as I looked at the Celestial Being's body, seething at how she had passed.

But then I closed my eyes, attempting to calm down.

I had to avoid losing my temper.

I breathed deeply, before looking at the thorns that were engulfing the Ethereal City.

But that just made my blood boil even more.

The other Archangels in the Afterworld, they had to know about this, about the chaos that was going on in the Ethereal City.

About everything.

About the bones of the dead Beings.

About the thorny vines that had taken over the grounds.

And then this, the death of a Celestial Being who had pricked her finger.

I had to talk to the Archangels about this, but then again, I had to talk with them anyway, since I had to bring the Being to the Afterworld.

Bring her to the Heavens to protect her from Eternal Damnation.

I took a breath through my lungs, before I carefully made my way toward the deceased Being.

I closed my eyes, bowing my head low, and touched her arm.

I said the incantation. The words were of a different tongue, and that was when her body evaporated.

I knew then that she was in the Afterlife.

36

Acanthus

I landed on a branch, still in the form of a bat.

Right near the mouth of the cave, where the Minotaur was, but then I blinked, confused.

I didn't see the Aureate Doe anywhere.

I flew toward the ground, shifting quickly so that I wouldn't get attacked by the Minotaur.

But I couldn't see the Doe.

I entered the mouth of the cave, only to see the blood-red eyes of the Beast.

The glittering body was nowhere to be seen.

She had run away.

I gritted my teeth together as I seethed.

My muscles tensed, and my hands turned into fists.

I growled before I punched the wall of the cave with all my strength, and then I brought my fist back to my side, only to see dirt and blood on my knuckles.

I snarled, pushing past the pain that radiated from my hand.

But then I just exhaled, a growl in my throat.

The Aureate Doe had escaped.

Celio

"Celio?"

I turned to see Chrysanthe nearby, away from the thorny brambles that were engulfing the ground.

My wings flapped as I flew to her, my heart rate already calming as I saw her.

"I need to go up to Heaven," I told her. "I must make sure the Archangel who died is in the Afterlife, and also, I need to talk to Beacon and Nevaeh. They need to know about what just happened. I'll be careful, I promise," I finished, kissing Chrysanthe. "I promise," I repeated as Chrysanthe nodded, but then I heard a wild, feral bellow.

Right behind me.

All three of us: Sybella, Chrysanthe, and I twisted our bodies around to look at the creature, and another bellow escaped from its body as it landed, hitting the ground of the Ethereal City.

It landed away from the vast area, where the vines and thorns and poison had taken over.

Chrysanthe gasped, as the Oracle and I were just watching the animal. Chrysanthe blinked several times, and then realized what it was, as well as where it lived.

"What is it, Chrysanthe?" I asked.

"It's a Peryton," she said. "A hybrid creature that has the head, neck, forelegs, and antlers of a stag, while it also has the plumage, wings, and hindquarters of a large bird. The animal is from the Aerial Alpines."

I saw Chrysanthe squint, saw her notice how agitated and nervous the Peryton was, when the Oracle went up to it.

She put her hand on the stag's body.

The movement made the Peryton calm down, all while she was trying to understand what was going on with the stag-like creature.

The Oracle closed her eyes, before immediately opening them again.

The Peryton let out a snort.

Sybella looked at Chrysanthe and I, and had an alarmed expression on her face. "The Peryton lives in the Aerial Alpines with Cyra, and the Aureate Doe. The Peryton, he is trying to alert us," she stated.

But then the Oracle looked straight at both Chrysanthe and I, dead in the eyes.

"The Aureate Doe, she has been taken from the Aerial Alpines. She has been taken from Cyra."

38

Chrysanthe and I looked at each other.

"I have to go. I need to see Beacon and Nevaeh, tell them what has been going on. On top of everything else," I said quickly.

It was going to be a lot to discuss with the sibling Archangels, but I had to speak to them.

I kissed Chrysanthe gently before I expanded my black wings out from my back, flying toward the Heavens.

39

Chrysanthe

I watched Celio leave, my heart feeling like it was trapped in my throat.

The Peryton was still beside Sybella and I, and was getting extremely agitated and nervous.

I looked worriedly at the stag-like animal, when I heard a familiar snort, followed by a whinny.

But then I heard a familiar bleat as well; I turned around to see Maximus, the Winged Horse, and the…the… Aureate Doe.

I blinked several times as I saw both animals, although I could see the Doe was covered in numerous cuts and scrapes all over her jeweled, golden hide.

She also was limping.

I leaned down to pet her, and that was when a soft bleat left her throat.

I saw the Peryton run up to the Aureate Doe, and within moments, the animal seemed instantly relaxed.

He rubbed his head into the Aureate Doe's neck affectionately, and I smiled.

But my expression didn't last long as I became rigid.

I was seeing just how torn up the Aureate Doe actually was.

I blinked in immediate surprise, but then turned to the pitch-black Winged Horse that was still waiting for me.

I walked over to the stallion, brushing his mane and ears, before he bowed, letting me get on him.

Like before, when I got on Maximus, I grasped his mane, holding on tightly.

He reared up on his hind legs, flapping his wings, and then galloped off.

Maximus reached the end of the Ethereal City before flying off.

Flying off and headed to the Aerial Alpines.

Again.

40

Acanthus

I still was in the cave with the Minotaur. He was snoring loudly while lying on the bones of the dead.

The Celestial Beings who had been eaten by him.

I went to the entrance of the cave, and as I went outside, I began pacing back and forth, my head down as a growl rumbled through my throat.

Irritated by the fact the Aureate Doe had escaped, and I couldn't get to the Enchanted Powder to destroy Phoenix.

I decided to go to visit the Seer Sisters who had told me what I had needed to do.

The Aureate Doe had run away, I couldn't get to the Enchanted Powder to destroy Phoenix, and the Utopian Sword was nowhere to be found.

I quickly morphed into a crow, flying over to the swamp to speak to the Seer Sisters once more.

I morphed back into myself before I realized I had forgotten payment to give to Levana and Morana.

Everything I was told by the Sisters had not happened, so I didn't think I needed payment.

Instead, I walked over to the tent where Levana and Morana lived.

The Seer Sisters heard me coming, and I saw them climbing slowly out of the tent.

They were visibly nervous encountering me once more, and I heard them swallowing loudly before they spoke.

"Hi, Acanthus. How can we help you?"

41

Celio

I landed in the Afterworld, extending my black wings out as I hit the ground.

I found Beacon and Nevaeh outside the Divine Castle.

"Beacon? Nevaeh?"

They heard their names, turning quickly, simultaneously.

Both of their faces lit up. I could tell they were ecstatic to see me.

Both ran up before locking me in a bear hug.

Nevaeh was on my left, while Beacon was on my right. Nevaeh began to cry into my shoulder.

"When we saw the Archangel's body, we thought you were the victim," she said thickly, blubbering into my shoulder.

Beacon hugged me tightly.

I just smiled as they pulled away from me. I looked both in the eyes.

"Thank you so much. I missed you both," I said, before taking a deep breath to steady myself.

Nevaeh and Beacon waited patiently as I gathered myself together.

It was after a few moments that I spoke.

"The Being from the Abyss killed the Archangel who showed up here, in the Afterworld," I said momentarily, glancing around, trying to find her.

Beacon noticed the way I was acting, my body language, and that was when he spoke.

"Celio, she's safe. The body of the Archangel is protected. She's not going to face Eternal Damnation."

I took in Beacon's words before I continued talking.

"When we went to the Aerial Alpines- Chrysanthe and I- we got the Fire Ruby from the Aureate Doe and spoke to Cyra. Chrysanthe has the Ruby now, but unfortunately, the Doe has been stolen from Cyra and the Aerial Alpines."

The moment I said that, Nevaeh and Beacon's eyes grew wide.

"Acanthus, he took her," Nevaeh said.

I nodded silently, agreeing with her, while Beacon just gulped.

"Yes, he did," I said. "And now, we must get her back to Cyra. The Peryton living in the Aerial Alpines came to the Ethereal City as well. Sybella figured out what was going on, and then the Aureate Doe showed up on the grounds of the Ethereal City. She showed up battered, bruised, and limping. Which means that possibly, Acanthus was harming her."

I took a deep breath before continuing.

"Chrysanthe has the Fire Ruby, but what do we do now that Acanthus has stolen the Doe and poisoned the Ethereal City with lethal plants?"

Nevaeh and Beacon glanced at each other momentarily, before Beacon spoke.

"You must get to the Ethereal City as fast as possible; you must go and talk to Phoenix. He can help you, and he also has the Enchanted Powder that can defeat both the Minotaur and Acanthus. Phoenix has most of the Powder, but I think that Acanthus somehow found some of it, and then used it on Cyra and the Aureate Doe."

Beacon paused to take a breath, and then continued.

"Go to Phoenix, find the Enchanted Powder, and after that, we- Nevaeh, Chrysanthe, you, and I- will all go to the Heavenly Falls and talk with Hali again."

Beacon stopped for a moment, looking at me, making sure that I understood everything that I'd been told.

I nodded.

"I understand," I said. "I got it."

42

Chrysanthe

Maximus' wings flapping caused air to rush onto my cheeks, tickling my skin as he flew higher and higher into the atmosphere.

I held on tightly to his mane as we flew to the Aerial Alpines.

I saw a break in the clouds after what felt like seasons, and finally was able to see the sun scattering light among the rocky landscape.

Maximus lowered himself to the ground as I saw Cyra in a portion of the mountainous area.

She was incredibly distraught, crying beyond belief.

Maximus got even lower as he approached the ground, and it was once he hit the terrain with his back hooves that I saw Cyra's eyes on the Winged Horse and I.

Like I knew Maximus would do, the stallion threw his wings out, reared up, and then landed on all four hooves, a loud whinny escaping his throat.

I smiled.

Maximus certainly loved to show off.

I continued to grin as I dismounted, but the expression changed quickly as I looked at Cyra, who appeared visibly distraught.

I went over to her side, grasping her hands in order to get her attention.

"Cyra," I started as tears began to flood her eyes. "Cyra, the Aureate Doe is safe."

"But... but... the Being from Hell, he took her from me. How can she be safe?"

"She's in the Ethereal City right now. If Acanthus had her and took her away from you, then somehow, she escaped. The Doe is safe now. The Oracle is keeping watch over her."

Cyra blinked, taking a deep breath, and exhaled slowly.

"She's okay, I promise," I told her.

I watched her as she began to calm herself down. I asked her how the Being from the Abyss stole the Aureate Doe.

She blinked before she spoke.

"He used the Enchanted Powder. He paralyzed me with it, threw it on the Doe as well, shapeshifted into a black hawk, and ripped her up by grabbing her with extremely sharp talons. I was screaming as the Doe was taken away..."

Tears started to form in Cyra's eyes again, but I took her hand once more.

"I will defeat Acanthus and bring the Doe back to you. I promise."

Cyra looked me in the eyes, a tear running down her cheek.

"Okay, Chrysanthe. Okay."

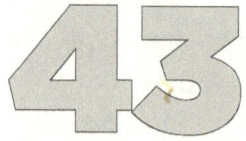

Acanthus

The Seer Sisters shuffled their feet as they looked at me.

Both of them- Levana and Morana- took nervous, deep breaths.

I walked up to the siblings, stopping right in front of them before I spoke.

"I have an issue, Seer Sisters," I grumbled unhappily.

Levana wore the headpiece so she could see me clearly, while Morana remained blind.

Levana shifted her weight absently.

There was a terrified look in her eyes.

"What is it?" she asked me.

"I can't get to the Enchanted Powder anymore, and the Aureate Doe has run off. How else can I get to the Abyss? How else would I go to the Underworld?"

I clenched my teeth and fists together.

"Tell me the truth, Seer Sisters," I growled as I watched them.

Morana touched Levana's shoulder blindly.

"Give me the headpiece, Levana," Morana said. "Let me speak to him."

Levana brought her attention to her sister, turning away from me, before taking the bull-skull and placing it on Morana's head.

It took only a moment, but her eyes changed from milky-white and clouded, to green irises with black pupils.

Morana took another breath before looking me in the eyes.

"Have you found the Utopian Sword, Acanthus?" she asked, to which I silently shook my head.

"Well, you must get the other half of the Sword. Chrysanthe has the other, smaller, piece. The other piece is called the Empyrean Blade, as you hopefully know. Acanthus, you must find the Aureate Doe, capture Phoenix-either by using more of the Enchanted Powder, or by finding Chrysanthe-in order to get the Empyrean Blade. Those are the only ways the Inferno River can be opened, in order to get to the Abyss. As we told you before."

Morana took a breath before continuing.

"But, in order to open up the way to Hell, you *at least* have to find the Utopian Sword, and kill a creature or Being with pure qualities. The mixture of your blood, mixed with pure blood, will open up the entranceway to the Underworld."

I saw Morana look at me, dead in the eyes, making sure that I understood what she had been telling me.

"So, I must get the Empyrean Blade by finding Chrysanthe, and also get ahold of the Utopian Sword," I said.

I was still aggravated that the Aureate Doe ran off, and that I was locked out of the Elysian Manor.

I gritted my teeth just thinking about it.

But then I looked at Morana, who was still watching me closely.

"Thank you for the information, Seer Sisters," I said.

I quickly morphed into a bat and flew away from the swamp.

I left the Seer Sisters behind.

Celio

I flew as fast as I could back to the Ethereal City.

The Elysian Manor was within my sights when I got there, and I immediately went over to the castle-like residence, knocking on the door, waiting anxiously for someone to respond.

Someone finally did, and that was when I asked if there was any payment needed to see and or talk to Phoenix.

I had never met Phoenix before.

All I knew was that he was the oldest Celestial Being to exist.

The Being who answered the door nodded at my words, and then allowed me to come inside the Elysian Manor.

The Elysian Manor was gigantic as I stepped inside.

I followed the Being up to one of the chambers, and stopped when they paused to speak with someone.

Then he turned around, looking at me.

"Celio here wants to go see Phoenix, but he doesn't have any payment. Could you please tell him what he will need?"

Both Beings, they brought their attention to me, and that was when I took a deep breath.

"There is a lot of destruction going on here, in the Ethereal City, and in the Afterworld. The Minotaur and the Hell Being need to be stopped. They have to be. I must go see Phoenix. I must."

The Being nearby began to speak, and then just opened a drawer in a dresser that he was beside.

"Well, if you must go see Phoenix, you are going to need this. You will need payment. It's expensive where you're going."

The Being tossed me a coin; I glanced down to see what it was.

It was an orange coin with a phoenix, wreathed in flames.

I turned the coin around in my hand before I put it in my palm, making a fist.

I brought my hand to the side, and then looked at both Beings in front of me.

"Thank you. Both of you."

I said it partially absentmindedly, turning the coin around once more in my hand.

"You're welcome," they responded. "You're very welcome."

45

Chrysanthe

aximus flew to the Ethereal City; I had just arrived when I saw Celio walk out of the Elysian Manor. I dismounted the Winged Horse, going up to my love, and hugging him before he spoke in my ear.

"We must go see Phoenix, Chrysanthe. We have to put a stop to this, and find a way to get rid of the destruction to the Realm."

He looked at the poisonous plants, unnerved by their appearance, when a Celestial Being approached us and said, "Phoenix could help destroy the vines. Flames will kill the plants, and also harm the Hell Being, since that is his Fate Tattoo."

Celio and I just stared at him, blinking as we took in the Being's words.

I spoke.

"Well, we must go see Phoenix, then. We must rid the Realm and the Afterworld of evil."

I looked up at a castle-like structure in the atmospheric 'sky.'

I had always been told by the Oracle where Phoenix lived, so I knew exactly where to go.

I nudged Celio, and he turned toward me.

"Come on, my love. We must go see Phoenix."

46

&ven from the grounds of the Ethereal City, Phoenix's residence was impressive.

He was on a floating island near the City, and the castle-like structure was red and orange colored, while the main residence was ink black.

It was very interesting to see, and both Celio and I were taken aback by the sheer scope of it.

I blinked, coming back to myself, before I peered over at Celio, who smiled.

He leaned forward, kissing me, and then swiftly picked me up, holding me in his arms.

I grinned, and his black wings erupted out of his back.

And he flew to Phoenix's home.

Celio gently placed me on the ground as we reached the residence.

I smiled before the door opened, and Phoenix appeared in the entranceway.

Celio only had to knock once before the oldest Celestial Being in existence was right in front of us.

Phoenix had a Fate Tattoo of red-orange flames snaking down both of his arms, while he had another Tattoo on his chest, one that was of a Phoenix.

The flames of the creature extended over his heart.

His black, low-cut shirt partially covered the design of the flaming bird, but the flames on Phoenix's chest were visible on his skin, poking out from under his garment.

He also had light-colored shorts on.

Phoenix's brown eyes watched Celio and I, and then he squinted.

I could tell by his facial expression that he knew why Celio and I had come to see him.

And then he opened the door wide, allowing Celio and I to enter.

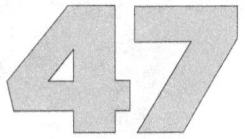 

Acanthus

I was disguised as a bat as I flew back to the cave.

I shifted into myself, pondering how to find Chrysanthe.

I paced back and forth outside the cave until I suddenly stopped.

The Oracle.

The Oracle was incredibly special to Chrysanthe.

She helped train Chrysanthe to be... be the... I had to swallow back the bile that rose through my throat.

The Protector of the Earth.

I would have to find the Oracle if I wanted to find Chrysanthe.

Finding the Oracle was not only the way to get to Chrysanthe and find the Empyrean Blade, it was also going to be the way that I could torture the Oracle.

Sybella had thrown Thana in the Inferno River as an infant, leaving her to drown and become the Queen of the Damned.

I gritted my teeth together at the mere thought.

But then I relaxed, knowing that Thana would be avenged eventually, and that I would meet up with her in the Abyss.

48

Chrysanthe

elio and I entered Phoenix's residence, which was gigantic. We both marveled at the sheer size of his home when Phoenix turned around to look at us.

He could tell we were both shocked.

"I designed this residence myself," he said as we looked at him. "It took a while to figure out the way I wanted everything to look."

My eyes drifted away from my surroundings so that I watched Phoenix.

"Well, your living quarters are incredible," I said, and from beside me, out of my peripheral vision, I saw Celio nodding in agreement.

Throughout the home was a mixture of orange-red colors, surrounded by a black background.

It mimicked what Phoenix looked like at the current moment, with his orange-red Fate Tattoos which resembled flames, and his black shirt.

Phoenix cleared his throat, and the noise brought me back to the present.

"I know the Oracle has told you about me, about how I can defeat both threats to the Afterworld, and the Ethereal City. She is correct, I can help you, but I must tell you that morphing into a phoenix constantly has caused me to grow weaker. I must have the Fire Ruby if I am to help you both," he told us softly.

I dug into the bag over my shoulder and pulled out the stone. "I was able to get the Ruby."

Phoenix nodded approvingly as I gave the stone to him.

"Thank you, Chrysanthe," he told me. "Now that I have the Fire Ruby, I can help you, and hopefully we can restore the peace to the Realms."

Acanthus

I growled as I thought about both Chrysanthe and the Oracle.

My teeth ground together, and I snarled.

I thought about seeing the two cradles.

One was for Chrysanthe, which appeared all fantastic and lovely with her name painted on it, while the other one was black and bare of any name.

There was nothing on the second cradle that signified the baby would be loved, respected, or cared for.

And I knew who was to blame for that.

The Oracle.

I began to walk away from the cave, where the Minotaur was sleeping.

After a few steps away from the cave, I took a deep breath before shifting into a wolf.

And then I ran through the woods, bolting over to the nearby Ethereal City.

50

I felt my blood boil as the thought came to me about how Thana was treated.

I was unable to get control over my anger, and I snarled as I morphed into the wolf.

I ran to the edge of the woods to where the Ethereal City began.

I was pleased to see my Fate Tattoo engulfing the City.

But that was the only thing that I was pleased about.

Now, I had to find the Oracle.

Find the Oracle, get to Chrysanthe, and force her to give up the Empyrean Blade, as well as give up the location of the Utopian Sword.

Once I was able to do that, I was going to feed the Oracle to the Minotaur, kill Chrysanthe, and open the entranceway to the Underworld.

Still in wolf form, my fur stood up on end, especially near the nape of my neck.

I growled before walking into the Ethereal City, finding the shadowy area of the Celestial Realm, and going over to the bones of the dead Beings.

I prowled around in the darkness, my paws crunching on the remains, before I just sat down in the mixture of skeletal fragments.

I waited there, waited for the Oracle to finally appear.

Appear so that I could eventually open the Inferno River, and go to Hell.

Go to Hell, and see Thana again.

51

Chrysanthe

hoenix morphed into the flame-engulfed bird and sat on his perch. He took the Fire Ruby and placed it in the ashes below him.

They were the remains of himself.

He sighed, and within moments, the Ruby got sucked into the ashes, being pulled underneath.

I gasped; Phoenix turned and peered into my eyes.

"The ashes ate the Ruby up," he said. "I really needed that; I was getting weaker."

He seemed to trail off, but then looked back at me after a few moments. "But now I have the stone. I will be able to assist you and help vanquish the threats."

Phoenix looked first at me, and then at Celio. He stared at the both of us, before saying, "The Minotaur has created too much havoc, and destroyed so much in the Ethereal City and the Afterworld, that the creature *must* be killed. Since the Hellion brought the Minotaur with him from the Abyss, the Beast must be eliminated."

He paused to take a breath, and then continued.

"It cannot wreak anymore havoc. Destroying the Minotaur will be the best way to defeat Acanthus. It will make the Hell Being vulnerable so that he will be stopped. Trap the Minotaur, kill it, and that is the best way to make Acanthus weak."

I stared at Phoenix, watching him carefully.

"So, how would we be killing the Minotaur? Or would we just be using the Empyrean Blade?" Celio questioned.

Phoenix's hair began to smoke.

His Fate Tattoo partly became real flames.

Phoenix watched Celio for a moment, before answering him.

"The Utopian Sword is the way to defeat both the Minotaur and Acanthus."

Acanthus

I was startled awake by bones crunching, only to realize I had fallen asleep on the skeletal fragments.

I was still in my wolf form, and woke up snarling at the fact that I'd fallen asleep.

I quickly got up and ran into the woods, when I saw her.

The Oracle.

I saw the Oracle fly off in her Being form.

Her long blond hair reached her elbows, while she was in a green dress, with giant black wings erupting from her back.

I watched her carefully, my yellow eyes blazing.

I growled, my throat rumbling as I watched Sybella from afar.

The shadowy area I was in was really the morgue of the Ethereal City.

No Celestial Being wanted to come here, at least the Pure Beings, since the morgue was cursed.

It was cursed by the Minotaur because the Beast ate the Beings, and the remains were untouchable.

I watched the Oracle steadily as she unknowingly flew above the trees and the forest, climbing higher and higher into the sky, before she flipped forward in the air.

A bright light surrounded her, and that was when she transformed into the barn owl.

I growled, the sound ripping through my chest cavity, and shivered as I morphed once more.

This moment though, I changed into a vulture before flying away, following the Oracle as she flapped her wings; she climbed higher and higher into the atmosphere, not knowing that I was right behind her.

Chrysanthe

My eyes widened as I heard Phoenix's words. I blinked for several moments, and then looked at Celio, who was as taken aback as I was.

"The Utopian Sword?" he asked.

Phoenix nodded silently.

"The Utopian Sword is part of the Empyrean Blade. It- meaning the Utopian Sword- needs to be melded together with the Blade. Either an Archangel or Hali can do that," Phoenix said. "The Minotaur can be killed with the Sword. The creature has harmed way too many Celestial Beings, and has tasted blood. The Beast must be eliminated. Its blood can then open up the Heavenly Falls."

"The Heavenly Falls will treat our wounds, as well as the wounds of my parents, correct?" I asked.

Phoenix nodded.

"Yes, Chrysanthe. That is correct."

54

I looked at Phoenix, and that was when I felt a hand on my shoulder, and I knew automatically that it was Celio.

"So, the Utopian Sword is in the Afterworld, right?" I asked.

Phoenix nodded.

"Yes, it is being protected in the Heavenly Falls."

I nodded understandingly.

"Okay, Phoenix. Thank you for telling us about all of this. I really appreciate it.

"You're welcome, Chrysanthe. You're welcome."

Acanthus

I landed on a tree branch still morphed into the vulture, watching the Oracle as she was perched on a branch nearby.

I waited patiently as she was cleaning her feathers, completely unaware that she was being watched.

I clacked my beak menacingly, and flew off, catching Chrysanthe's former mentor by surprise.

The Oracle turned her barn owl head around, looking at me, but she didn't get off the branch fast enough.

I caught the Oracle; she let out a screech of agony as my talons dug into her feathered body and wings.

There was nothing she could do though as she was in my talons.

I let out a sickening, terrifying scream as I flew away.

Now I could feed the Minotaur, and eventually get the ability to go to the Underworld, unlocking the way to Hell.

56

Chrysanthe

I looked at Phoenix before glancing at Celio. Then I brought my attention back to Phoenix.

"Okay, so we must find the Utopian Sword, at least, the other half, the other half being the Empyrean Blade?"

Phoenix nodded.

"Yes. Also, I will help you defeat Acanthus. I will set fire to the venomous vines that are still here, in the Ethereal City. He will be weakened by then, since the spiked vines are actually his Fate Tattoo. The only way to get blood from the Minotaur and Acanthus is to use the Utopian Sword."

Phoenix looked at Celio before he started talking to him.

"Celio, you are going to have to go to the Heavens and speak with Beacon and Nevaeh, they will meld the Empyrean Blade to the other half of the Celestial weapon."

Phoenix then turned to me.

"Chrysanthe," he said, glancing at the top of the handle that was the Empyrean Blade, in my skin disguised as a tattoo. "You are going to have to give Celio the Empyrean Blade before he goes to the Afterlife."

I turned my attention to Celio.

I scraped at my chest with my fingernails, before pulling the Blade from my flesh.

The Celestial object left my flesh within a moment, and I handed Celio the Blade; he carefully put it into his skin.

Celio and I both turned our attention to Phoenix once more.

"Celio, you have to go to the Afterworld now. Go there and let the Archangels know what has been happening. They need to meld the two parts of the weapon and give you the enchanted sword before you come back. "

Celio nodded and then looked away from Phoenix, glancing over at me.

"Alright," he said, acknowledging Phoenix's words as he watched me.

He then took a few steps toward me, kissing me softly, before he whispered into my lips.

"I'll be back, I promise," he said softly.

It was after that that he turned around, opening up the front entranceway to Phoenix's home.

Celio rolled his shoulders forward, releasing his black angel wings, and then flew away.

Celio was headed to Heaven.

Again.

Celio

I flew to the Afterworld, intent on speaking with Beacon and Nevaeh about all the topics that were told to me by Phoenix. I finally reached the Heavens after several moments of flying through the atmosphere. I was ready to talk with the siblings. I saw Serenity near the Divine Castle.

Serenity was the former Floating Soul who helped Chrysanthe and I on the trek to defeat Thana.

She was no longer a Floating Soul, and had on a beautiful, vibrant dress; her long brown hair cascaded past her shoulders.

Happiness seemed to radiate from her, even in her body language. She seemed ecstatic to be in the Heavens, and to not be a Floating Soul anymore.

Serenity blinked when she turned around and saw me, and in about two moments, she ran up to me, giving me a cordial hug.

"Hi, Celio," she said, a smile on her face. "It's really nice to see you again." Serenity spoke honestly, but then her eyebrows furrowed in confusion. "Where's Chrysanthe? Is she with you? Or is she on Maximus and heading over here? I know you both have another long journey that is quite the undertaking."

I shook my head.

"No, Chrysanthe isn't here at the moment, and she's not coming, at least, not yet. I mean, she's not following me here."

Serenity's eyebrows furrowed again, and that was when I spoke once more.

"I was told to come here by Phoenix. He wanted me to speak to Nevaeh and Beacon. Would you know where they are, Serenity?"

She blinked and then turned to the Divine Castle that was behind her. She met my eyes again and then nodded.

"Yes, I do, Celio. Come with me; they are in the Castle. I'll bring you to them."

I nodded.

"Thank you, Serenity," I said with a smile.

"You're welcome."

And I followed her into the residence of the Archangels.

58

Chrysanthe

I was in the Elysian Manor, and by now, it was nightfall.
I had spoken to Phoenix about my mother and father both being on Earth, and being unable to come back to the Afterlife.

Unable to come back without being caught in the Everlasting Light in Heaven and burning up.

The conversation I'd had with Phoenix kept cycling in my head, and kept me awake as I tossed and turned as I attempted to sleep.

But I couldn't.

The thoughts of my parents and Phoenix kept circulating inside my mind.

I thought about Celio going to the Afterworld, Viro and Thera being burned up in the Everlasting Light, the Minotaur and Acanthus obliterating both the Afterworld and the Ethereal City…

There was just a lot circulating in my brain.

Acanthus

I was still in the form of the vulture as I flew into the wooded area where the cave was.

I still had the Oracle in my talons, but she was rendered unconscious. I carelessly dropped her body in front of the bleak-looking lair, and I heard the deep guttural rumble meaning the Minotaur was inside.

And he must have been hungry.

The sun had set, and the sky was darkening as nightfall took over the atmosphere.

The growl that erupted from the Minotaur made me shiver as I flew away.

I abruptly morphed right into my Being form, before walking back to the Beast and the Oracle, who was still passed out.

Sybella was breathing; she just wasn't waking up.

A snarl erupted as the Minotaur watched the Oracle with his blood-red eyes.

His huge black body appeared incredibly strong and menacing as he turned to me.

He looked at Sybella, whose feathered body was covered in cuts and scrapes.

She was a mixture of ripped flesh and blood.

She was a mixture of gore.

My lip curled up in a snarl as the Minotaur turned his attention to the Oracle's bloody battered body.

He walked up to her, ready to grab her, when Sybella blinked, becoming conscious again.

She slowly came to her senses, and screeched as she saw the Minotaur leaning over her.

She, in her frightened state, partially lifted her body up by flying, but she screamed again since she was hurting.

Despite this, the Oracle lifted herself off the dirt, desperate to get away.

The Minotaur growled at her, sending shivers down my spine, and he attempted to bite her, but the Oracle quickly threw her weight forward.

To my horror, her talons sank into the Minotaur's face, causing him to stumble backward.

A loud, feral rumble sliced through his throat as I screamed in blistering anger.

The Oracle got away from the Beast, and I saw her fly higher and higher in the sky, narrowly missing the rock I threw at her.

Blood trickled down her feathered body as she flew away, and a piercing shriek escaped her.

The screech cut through the silence and the darkness of the night, but I was fuming, feeling as if my head was going to explode.

Yet another creature had escaped from my grasp.

Chrysanthe

A wild, piercing scream sliced through the nighttime silence, causing my eyes to immediately open.

I quickly clambered out of the sheets that were suddenly constrictive, and instantly went to the window.

The Oracle was flying around in her barn owl form, and I gasped when I saw her bloody, raw, shifted body.

The feathers on her were either falling off because of the wounds or were nonexistent.

I was completely taken aback.

I'd seen nothing like this, the violent look on Sybella's barn owl body was jarring.

Especially because the cuts and scrapes were on the Oracle, of all Beings.

I blinked for several moments, nonplussed, before I quickly threw on a shawl that I'd found nearby.

I bolted down the hallway, and instantly went to the entrance of the Elysian Manor, yanking the door open and going outside in the cool air.

The chill breeze sent a shiver down my spine, cutting through my body like an invisible blade.

I blinked in surprise at the sensation, pulling the shawl closer to myself so I wouldn't freeze.

Sybella turned her head, and looked straight at me from where she was perched.

She flew toward me.

Blood was all over her as she did so, dripping from her body, and I could hear her whimper in her barn owl form.

My heart partially broke just hearing her.

"Come on, Sybella," I said, pulling my shawl closer as I retreated to the door which was still open. "Come on in, Sybella. Let's get you healed."

And the Oracle flew into the Elysian Manor, her beak chattering from the wind.

61

Celio

Serenity and I were walking in the Divine Castle for only a moment or two before she stopped, smiling at Nevaeh. Her brother was nearby, and she nudged Beacon when she saw me.

Beacon smiled as he saw Serenity and I, and they quickly walked over to us.

They greeted Serenity cordially, before they both engulfed me in a massively strong bear hug.

The hug hurt a little, but I welcomed the sensation.

It was better to be loved than not to be cared about.

When they both loosened their grips, they appeared confused.

Beacon's eyebrows furrowed as the expression took over, and then he spoke.

"What has arisen now, Celio?" he asked. Beacon just watched my face, while Nevaeh gulped. "What is the issue now?"

I took a breath, releasing it out of my lungs, before I spoke.

"Phoenix told me to get back here and talk to the both of you. He said that Beacon," I brought my eyes over to him, "you can help me meld the other half of the Utopian Sword. Chrysanthe had the Empyrean Blade, but she had to give it to me so I could give it to you."

I looked at Beacon, who nodded.

"Okay," he said understandingly. "The thing is," Beacon said, sighing before continuing. "I don't have the other half of the Utopian Sword, at least, not inside the Divine Castle. Hali- the water sprite we met- she has the Sword. It is protected in the Heavenly Falls. We will have to talk to her about this predicament."

Beacon took a breath, and then continued.

"If you get the Utopian Sword and defeat Acanthus and the Minotaur, then you will reach your ultimate goal. Which is to save Chrysanthe's parents, and heal both of your wounds-Chrysanthe's and your own- since all of you were treated horribly by Thana. You all had something awful happen to you by the Queen of Death's hand. Once you defeat the Beast and Acanthus with the Sword, you'll be able to unlock the Water in the Heavenly Falls, and save everyone that you wish to save."

Beacon watched me steadily, and I knew that he was making sure that I heard him right.

Which I did.

"Thank you, Beacon," I told him.

But then I had another question that I'd just thought of.

"Beacon, how do I get the portion of the Sword from Hali?"

Beacon looked at me.

"Hali will help you. She'll cast an incantation to help you breathe underwater. Since she isn't the one defeating the threats, she isn't able to swim down and retrieve the Utopian Sword. All she can do is Guard the weapon, not get it and use it."

Beacon paused once more so that I could soak in what he was saying.

"Hali will help you obtain the Sword."

My heart began racing inside my chest. I'd never felt like I was under so much pressure in all of my existence.

Ever.

But I knew I had to do this.

To save everyone, and everything, I cared about.

ali's glittering, sheening water sprite body greeted us as we stood beside the Heavenly Falls.

Like before, Nevaeh had tossed a stone in the Water, causing it to ripple.

Moments later, Hali rose from the liquid, giving me a cordial nod before turning her attention to Beacon and Nevaeh. Hali peered around at all three of us before she spoke.

"Hello, Celio. Hello, Beacon, and Nevaeh. How can I help you?"

Nevaeh sighed, and said, "Celio needs to find the other half of the Utopian Sword. He already has half of it with the Empyrean Blade, but he needs the full complete weapon. We all know that you Guard it, so we all knew we needed to speak with you." Nevaeh sighed once she was done talking.

That was when I spoke up.

"I need your help, Hali. Sybella gave Chrysanthe the Empyrean Blade, which she then gave to me."

I glanced down for a moment to look at my chest, before I saw the Empyrean Blade Tattoo on my bare skin.

I saw Hali's eyes flicker to my body, before she looked back up at me.

"I will help you, Celio. I will help, but *you're* going to have to be the one that must *get* the Utopian Sword, is that understood?"

Hali looked at me steadily.

I nodded.

"Alright then. I will help you get the enchanted weapon."

I inhaled deeply, exhaling slowly as I entered the Water of the Heavenly Falls.

Hali swam up to me as soon as I did, putting her hand up to my throat.

I peered over at her arms, and realized that octopus tentacles were coiled around her flesh; her Fate Tattoo took over both of her extremities.

I focused on that as I felt her touch my neck.

I had entered the Heavenly Falls, but other Beings could only enter the Water if Hali had said an incantation.

An incantation that would protect both the Being and the Water, since the Falls were untouchable to any Being except Hali.

This was because Hali was the Guardian of the Falls.

She had said the incantation so that I could get into the enchanted Water, and then touched my skin.

I didn't stop her, since she appeared to know what she was doing, whatever it was.

It was to help me find and retrieve the other half of the Utopian Sword, I knew that.

So, I stayed silent.

"Do you know what I'm doing, Celio?"

I blinked, coming back to the present as I heard Hali's voice.

She was still concentrating, saying an incantation, as she gently put her extremities on my throat.

I took a breath before I spoke. "No. No, I don't, but I know that whatever you are doing, it is going to help me."

Hali chuckled, but then stopped, speaking again.

"Celio, lower yourself into the Water; become submerged."

"Do I have to wait until you take your hands off my throat?"

Hali shook her head. "No, I said an incantation, and now you have something special on you. You won't be able to breathe if I take my hands off your throat."

My heart skipped a beat in surprise. "Wait, what?"

Hali smiled, but then said, "Oh, you'll be able to hold your breath," she said, changing her mind about what she'd just told me. "Celio, go straight under the Water, right now."

She took her hands off my skin, and I instantly got submerged.

But then I felt movement on my flesh, like... like... there was something else on my neck now.

I felt my heart pummeling my chest, and I sucked in a breath in surprise.

Only to realize that... that... I could breathe.

I could breathe underwater.

I curiously touched my neck gingerly, and that was when I realized that... Hali had given me gills.

63

Chrysanthe

The Oracle was breathing hard as she landed on the wood table in the dining area.

I looked around, my eyebrows furrowing in both concern and sadness as blood dripped from Sybella's wings.

She let out a cry, wincing as she turned her body around, and that was when I saw a Celestial Being come from behind the corner with an expression on her face that mirrored mine.

She glanced at me, before peering back at Sybella, who closed her eyes in obvious pain.

I looked back at my former mentor.

"Sybella?" I asked. "Sybella, can you shift back into yourself? Can you morph?"

The Oracle moved her head, so that she was looking straight at me.

In her bird form, she sighed, blinking for several moments before shaking her head.

Even in her owl body, I could understand her.

Okay, I thought. *So, she can't even change back into her Being form.*

At that realization, my heart broke.

Sybella, you poor, poor thing.

But that was when I understood I had to heal her in her barn owl form.

She needed to shift so she could tell me what had happened.

But I knew, in the back of my mind, it was going to be a sad story.

I had to hear it, though; I had to know what was going on.

I brought my hands from my sides, rubbing them together in order to warm them up.

The inside of the Elysian Manor was still slightly cold from me opening up the entranceway.

A chill momentarily rattled my spine, and that was when I took a deep breath through my lungs.

I closed my eyes, breathing in and out.

In and out. In and out. In and out.

I kept my eyes closed for several moments afterward, going almost into a meditative state.

When my eyes opened once more, I felt incredibly relaxed.

Relaxed and clear-minded.

I caught Sybella looking at me in her bird form, her enormous eyes watching mine.

But then I just looked at her, growing calm as I brought my hands up to her torn flesh.

"Alright, Sybella," I told her as I focused on healing her. "Let's fix you up."

My former mentor was extremely wounded.

Extremely. Horribly.

It reminded me of when I healed Celio after he had been torn out of the Afterworld by Thana, when he got ripped up.

The sight of Sybella made me feel the same way. It all was sickening, the way she appeared.

Who would treat the Oracle this way?

Bile began to rise in my throat at just the carnage that was Sybella's barn owl body.

But I swallowed, determined to heal my former mentor the same way I had healed Celio.

Heat radiated through my palms as I touched the Oracle's bird form.

Her owl body was bloody beyond belief, but when I gently placed my hands on her, warmth circulated through my palms.

I carefully placed my hands on Sybella's wings, and the entirety of her feathered frame.

A cold sensation took over after the hot one, and within a few moments, the Oracle was healed.

She stared straight at me as her body got repaired.

A noise almost like the coo of a dove fluttered through her throat, and she stepped close to my face, rubbing her soft cheek into mine.

I laughed as the movement tickled my skin, and a smile made its way onto my lips.

"You feel better, don't you, Sybella?"

She clicked her beak together twice in response, and I giggled.

I took that as a yes.

Sybella rubbed her soft barn owl face on mine once more, and then flew to the side of the wood-grain table, a white light engulfing her as she moved quite a distance away from me.

Within moments, the barn owl completely disappeared, and Sybella was in her Being form. Her back was to me as she shifted into herself.

She slowly twisted her body around so she could face me, and smiled as her eyes connected with mine.

"Thank you, Chrysanthe," she said. "Thank you so much."

I grinned back at her.

"You're welcome, Sybella. You're welcome."

64

"What happened to you?" I asked, sitting at the long woodgrain table in the middle of the room.

I was sitting at the corner, while Sybella was at the end.

She sighed as I looked at her, my eyebrows creasing slightly in worry.

The Oracle's eyes immediately shifted to her hands, which were folded in her lap.

She then looked back up at me.

"Acanthus. It was Acanthus. He… he… has the ability to shapeshift, and he… he… was in the form of a vulture when… when… he flew over and grabbed me with his talons…"

My eyes grew wide.

That must've been agony.

Agonizing, as well as terrifying.

I sucked in a breath in both shock and horror as the Oracle just sat at the end of the table.

She just looked me straight in the eyes, nodding.

"The entire ordeal was absolutely terrifying." Sybella glanced at the floor, but then looked at me. "But now it's over and I was able to fly here and get healed with your help."

I blinked for several moments, and then shook my head, attempting to clear it.

"Well, I'm glad I saved you. I'm extremely glad."

Sybella and I spoke for a little while longer, staying in the dining area before I yawned.

The Oracle's lips went to the corners of her mouth as she smiled, before a yawn engulfed her as well.

"I think I have to go back to sleep," I said, stretching my arms out as I got up from the chair; Sybella copied me as I stood. "Alright, I'm going to go back to my room."

Sybella nodded.

"Okay. I can find an extra room. If I can't, I'll go to sleep in my bird form."

"Well, I'll talk to you later."

The Oracle smiled in response.

I turned and walked down the hall and into my room, climbing into the bed and falling asleep quickly.

My head was pounding as I slowly opened my eyes, blinking rapidly as I attempted to take in my surroundings.

But then...

I...I...

I realized I couldn't see anything in front of me.

In front of me, beside me, or behind me.

I was just engulfed in blackness when I awoke.

My breathing became rapid, but then I felt something soft against my right side.

I had the sensation of warmth beside me, but then there was a sound of a sharp whine that followed the feeling of softness.

My forehead and eyebrows crinkled in confusion, but then I heard panting, and felt a wet object on my cheek.

I turned to my left side immediately, and got up from the ground.

Scrambling, I ran toward the very tiny sliver of light that was visible.

I looked down at my hands, but that was when I felt my heart skip a beat.

My hair hung long, but it... it... was brown.

Brown, and when I turned my left wrist around to look at it, I saw... saw... an orange-yellow, disturbing looking skull tattooed on my wrist.

My Fate Tattoo was a skull.

A scary skull.

I tore my eyes away and looked up after a while of peering at my arm, and that was when I heard the panting once more.

I saw a massive black wolf the size of a horse.

The wolf was gigantic but emaciated, his teeth exposed because the flesh that was supposed to be protecting its muzzle had been torn away.

It took a few moments to realize that it was the wolf's wet tongue that had touched my cheek.

I began hyperventilating as I realized that I was no longer myself.

I was Thana.

I was the Queen of the Underworld...

My eyes opened instantly; my skin was soaked in sweat as I came to.

My mouth was agape as I was about to scream, but momentarily, I realized that it was just a dream.

It was just a dream.

I pushed myself up from the sheets, feeling them cling to my skin as sweat soaked my flesh.

I had no strength left in my frame. My body felt heavy.

I took a deep breath, and quickly realized I could barely move. It took all the power in me just to get out of bed.

When I looked in the nearby mirror, I saw myself, my peacock feather Fate Tattoos on my eyes, my blond hair that reached my elbows, and my chrysanthemum tattoo on my left hand and wrist.

The slip I was wearing covered my body, reaching my knees.

Overall, I still looked like myself.

I didn't look like my sister, not in the slightest.

I felt the tight, nervous wad of anxiety leave me as I saw my reflection, and I took a deep breath.

I wasn't my twin sister from Hell.

I was myself.

I wasn't Thana.

65

I sighed deeply as I lay in bed, my thoughts of my dream circulating in my brain.

I was not my twin sister. I would never be my twin sister. I was myself, and I lived on Earth, not in Hell.

I was the Protector of the Earth, and not the Queen of the Abyss.

I was myself.

I took another slow breath before I blinked, trying hard to calm myself down.

If only Celio was here, here with me…

I knew though, that he was in the Afterworld, talking to Beacon and Nevaeh.

He was going to get the Utopian Sword so I could defeat both Acanthus and the Minotaur.

I just lay on the bed in the Elysian Manor, thinking about my love, when finally, I just took the bedsheets off my body.

I clambered out of the bed, immediately going to the window, where I just stayed, looking at the sky.

I missed Celio so much…

I turned around, going to the front door of the room.

I opened it up, glancing once behind me, taking in the place where I'd slept before walking out of the Elysian Manor and into the cool, pitch-black early morning sky.

I whistled into the surroundings, when I heard a whinny, and then a flapping noise.

I smiled.

It was Maximus. I had succeeded in having him come to me.

I heard him before I saw him, his hooves hit the ground of the Ethereal City, and I heard him galloping before I saw him in the darkness.

There was just a sliver of light from one of the windows in the Elysian Manor that illuminated Maximus' black body.

The light was the only way that I could see the Winged Horse.

I saw the stallion, and whistled softly to him.

His ears perked up as he heard me, and then saw me, walking up as I slowly beckoned him forward with my hand.

Maximus paused once I put my palm straight out, right in his face.

"Whoa," I said gently. "Whoa, Maximus."

I heard a soft nicker radiate through his throat, and I smiled, petting his snout.

"Good boy, Maximus," I said as I continued to rub his fur. "Good boy."

He rubbed his snout into my abdomen, and I laughed.

"Okay, boy. Are you going to take me to the Afterworld? Can you?"

As if in response, the Winged Horse snorted.

Snorted, and then bowed.

A smile made its way on my lips, and the expression stayed on my mouth as I got on the stallion.

I gripped Maximus' mane tightly before clicking my tongue.

"Come on. Let's go to the Afterworld."

Maximus snorted, rearing up on his hind legs, and took off galloping before we were both airborne.

The wind whipped past my cheeks as he flew higher and higher into the sky.

We were headed to Heaven.

I felt Maximus descend, his frame moving downward as I held onto his mane.

He snorted as he landed on the ground of the Heavens, preening like always by throwing his wings upward.

It was almost like he was announcing his arrival.

I giggled as I dismounted, and I walked over to the Divine Castle; I saw the lights in one of the windows turn on, and I waited patiently before the entranceway to the Castle opened.

To my surprise, it was Serenity.

"Chrysanthe!" she yelled excitedly. "Chrysanthe, how are you?"

The former Floating Soul engulfed me in a bear hug instantly.

I smiled.

"Good, Serenity. I'm doing well."

She pulled away from me so that she could look into my face.

Her hair was long and brown, while her eyes were blue and appeared to sparkle.

She was radiating happiness as I looked at her.

She had a beautiful red dress on that complemented her frame.

"How about you, Serenity?"

She grinned.

"I'm doing excellent." She blinked, and then her eyebrows furrowed. "Did you want to see Celio? Is that why you came?"

I nodded.

Serenity scrunched her eyebrows as she thought about something.

"I'm sorry, Chrysanthe. Celio isn't inside the Divine Castle. He's in the Heavenly Falls with Hali."

Hali.

The water sprite who Guarded the Heavenly Falls.

So that was where the Utopian Sword was, hiding in the enchanted body of Water.

"Let me go get Beacon and Nevaeh. Or, one of them. Come in, Chrysanthe. You can come sit down while I look for them."

I grinned at Serenity, before looking at Maximus.

He threw his snout high in the air, flapping his wings as his chocolate brown eyes found mine.

I twisted back around afterward, following Serenity as she made her way to the entrance of the Divine Castle.

I sat in the chair that she gestured to, and then she spoke.

"I will be right back, okay?"

I nodded.

"Yes," I said.

Serenity walked off afterward, and I sat patiently, waiting for her to come back with Beacon, Nevaeh, or both of the Archangels.

I waited patiently for a while.

My right arm felt tender suddenly as I sat on the chair.

It was starting to bother me as I had been waiting for Serenity to come back.

The sensation in my limb was abruptly bothering me.

It was as if the blood flow had quickly left my extremity.

I shook my hand from side to side, trying to get rid of the sensation. But it wouldn't leave.

I winced. The feeling just wasn't going away.

In fact, it was getting worse.

Within mere moments, the slight bothering sensation became a stinging pain.

I winced again, but then I heard a gasp, followed by a shout.

"Chrysanthe! Chrysanthe, you have to get out of here!"

Sweat began to escape the pores of my skin as I began to feel weak, and I immediately felt woozy.

I struggled to stay upright as I began to stand, and that was when I fell into someone's arms, losing consciousness immediately.

66

"Chrysanthe? Chrysanthe, can you hear me?"

A voice swam into my ears as I came to.

It felt like I was a million miles away; I felt so groggy, but I slowly opened my eyes to see a face staring down at mine.

I blinked for several moments before I got my focus back, and I sat up. I jumped slightly as I saw Nevaeh staring down at me.

I inhaled quickly, backing up as I saw another familiar face.

Beacon. Beacon and Nevaeh.

Beacon and Nevaeh were looking at me.

"Where… where am I?" I asked them in my drowsy state. "Where… where…?"

It was Nevaeh who answered.

"We are on Earth," she said, glancing around at the surroundings.

I looked around, automatically seeing green grass, the blue sky, and bright yellow sunlight.

I squinted from the illumination.

"Are you feeling better?" Beacon asked.

The throbbing in my right extremity was gone, but now I felt unsteady, since I had just woken up.

But other than that, I felt alright.

I nodded, looking at Beacon as I did so.

"My arm feels better, but my head… I just feel out of it," I said, being truthful.

"Well, you lost consciousness, so I understand that," Beacon said. "You were saying your arm was hurting?"

He glanced down at my right extremity, where the tattoo of the map of my World was, intermingled with the scar from the Empyrean Blade.

The moment he did that, I gasped.

Wait a moment, I thought.

My mind went back to when Sybella had told me about the Everlasting Light that surrounded the Heavens, the Afterworld.

Sybella had said an incantation so that I wouldn't burn up in the Light of the Afterlife.

The reason being the scar.

The scar on my right arm.

I shook my head as I realized that was what had happened.

My scar was what had caused me to pass out, and it would've killed me if I stayed up in the Afterworld.

I would've burned up.

Beacon saw my expression change, and that was when I partially moved my arm in response to the confused look that was on his face.

But he understood within moments.

His mouth popped open in surprise, while Nevaeh started to speak.

"You were going to burn up in the Everlasting Light. Your scar alerted you." Nevaeh looked at my face before peering over at her sibling. "It's a good thing we found you."

A gulp resonated from my throat as I thought about what could've happened to me.

I would've… would've… died, without Beacon and Nevaeh's assistance.

My eyelashes fluttered as I blinked, pushing myself up as I brought my palms to the grass.

"Can you support your weight?" Beacon asked. "Or are you still woozy?"

I shook my head, and then said, "No, I'm not woozy. I want to go to my treehouse."

I glanced at the Archangel siblings, before looking at the green grass of the Earth. I brought my attention to my treehouse; I was near it.

It was behind me.

I wanted to go to my treehouse, as well as see Caliya.

A smile formed on my face just thinking about the tigress.

I put my bodyweight on both of my extremities, standing with no assistance from Beacon or Nevaeh.

I was woozy for a few moments as I stood up, but then I blinked, gathering my surroundings before I felt steady.

I twisted my body around, and I brought my eyes to my treehouse.

Not only did I see my treehouse, I also saw Caliya coming out of the woods.

A friendly rumble escaped her as she ran toward me.

I smiled as the happy noises shook through the tigress' muzzle, and I sighed, instantly relaxing.

Caliya flopped down on the green grass, her tail thrashing the air in her excited state. She exhaled.

I laughed as I saw her, and then I stroked her striped, intricately detailed fur, and she huffed, the air soaking my face. I continued to smile.

I loved Caliya. I loved her so much.

Celio

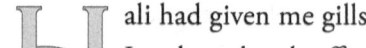

ali had given me gills.

I took my hands off my neck as I surfaced again, glancing at the Guardian of the Heavenly Falls.

A smile made its way on my lips.

"Thank you, Hali."

"You're welcome, Celio. Now, you can find the other half of the Utopian Sword." She glanced at my bare chest for a moment, before she looked back up at me. "You already have the Empyrean Blade in your skin, so that's a good start."

Hali watched my eyes, and then she spoke again.

I turned my attention to the Water of the Heavenly Falls, and then brought my attention to the sprite.

"Good luck, Celio. When you find the enchanted weapon, come back and see me. I'll remove the gills, okay?"

I nodded. "Okay," I said. "I understand."

"Alright," she responded. "Good luck."

And she disappeared, swimming away in the enchanted liquid.

I submerged myself under the Water, and the gills began fluttering in the process.

They felt strange as the fluid hit them.

It felt odd, weird, but I got used to the sensation quickly. I had no choice but to.

The weapon was buried in the depths of the Heavenly Falls.

I sighed underwater, causing bubbles to form. They floated up to the surface, disintegrating as I pushed myself through the liquid.

I swam, making my way through the coral and the seaweed, ready to complete the task that was given to me.

It took a while to find the other half of the Empyrean Blade.

It was buried in the sand at the bottom of the Heavenly Falls.

I spotted the other portion of the sharp sword poking out of the white sand.

A smile engulfed my face.

Now, the evil Hellion and Thana's Beast could finally be destroyed.

Chrysanthe

aliya's bodyweight shifted completely into mine as her affectionate moan shook through her frame.

I grinned as Caliya rubbed her soft fur against my skin; she was moving and rumbling for several moments as I scratched the top of her head, her ears.

The tigress exhaled as she pushed the top of her skull into my chin and neck.

I laughed, rubbing her ears before I turned around, seeing Beacon and Nevaeh grin at the sight of Caliya and I.

"Are you okay now, Chrysanthe?" Nevaeh asked, and I nodded.

"Yes, I am," I told her, all while Caliya was pushing up against me.

I smiled once more at the big cat's moan, and nodded at Beacon and Nevaeh.

"Okay, Chrysanthe. If everything is going well with you, we are going to go back up to the Afterworld."

Their thick black wings then erupted out of their backs.

They flew back up to the Heavens, leaving Caliya and I behind.

I winced as I moved my scarred right arm around, trying to see how much mobility I had in it without my extremity causing me pain.

My arm still slightly stung.

I breathed slowly, methodically, as I felt the stinging pain. It was bearable, but it still hurt.

It was irritating.

I sighed as I saw Caliya come up to me. I stroked her face, rubbing my fingers into her cheeks, and it was as if she was a giant kitten all over again.

Caliya shut her amber eyes, a content rumble shaking through her throat.

When she opened her eyes once more, she pushed her massive head into my palm.

"Aww, Caliya, thank you, honey. Thank you so much."

I stroked her striped cheeks before I brought my arms up in the air, stretching.

I glanced around the treehouse.

I stretched out my muscles, quickly making my bed, and I grinned as I saw Caliya stretch as well.

Her claws were extended as she did so, and yawned, showing her canines that were as sharp as knives.

Her amber eyes bore into mine, and a breath shook through her throat.

I smiled at her, and she came up to me; I stroked her fur, looking at my treehouse.

It was great to be back on Earth, where I belonged, but I wanted to get back to the Ethereal City and the Afterworld.

I needed to save the Realms, but I couldn't at the moment.

Not until the Oracle came down to Earth again, reciting the incantation to protect me from the Everlasting Light.

I couldn't go anywhere.

I had to stay on Earth.

I stared at the surroundings outside my window, my thoughts immediately going to Celio, who was in the Afterworld.

I took a deep breath through my lungs.

I hoped he was alright.

I missed my love so much.

Celio

I rose from the Water of the Heavenly Falls, the other portion of the Utopian Sword in my hand.

I could barely breathe because of the gills.

I started to panic when I heard a splash and turned around.

Hali was behind me, watching my eyes.

"Celio," she said. "I am going to remove the gills before you head back."

I started to advance toward her, and I watched her as she put her hands on my throat.

She spread her fingers out on my neck, her palm on my skin, and said an incantation.

Within mere moments, I felt the flesh of my throat move, becoming normal once more.

Hali brought her hands back to her sides with a small smile.

"Now, you may go to the Afterworld with the rest of the Utopian Sword. You can also, for safekeeping, put the piece you found into your flesh."

I glanced down at my chest where the Empyrean Blade was, and took the other sharp piece of the weapon. I pushed it slowly into my skin.

I watched as it slowly disappeared into my flesh.

Sure enough, the portion of the weapon and Empyrean Blade were both visible.

I looked over at Hali, who was just watching me silently.

After a few moments, she spoke.

"Now, all you have to do is meld the Utopian Sword together, and you and Chrysanthe can defeat the Hellions that are causing massive destruction. Good luck, Celio," Hali finished, and then she disappeared, bubbles rising to the top of the Water in her wake.

I turned around afterward, making my way over to dry land.

I felt my thick black wings erupt from my back, and I flew upward into the air, headed to the Afterworld so I could find Beacon and Nevaeh.

Find them, and meld the Utopian Sword together.

70

The Empyrean Blade and the Utopian Sword were safe in my skin as I flew from the Heavenly Falls.

I smiled as I landed on the ground of the Afterworld, the Realm that all Archangels called home.

I threw my black wings out as I looked around at my surroundings, before I saw Beacon walking outside the Divine Castle.

I called out his name, and he looked over at me, a giant smile on his face.

Beacon ran to me. "Celio," he said. "You're back." The Archangel gave me a quick friendly hug. "You have the other portion of the Empyrean Blade, I assume?"

I nodded.

"Yes, I do. Hali gave me gills so I could go to the bottom of the Heavenly Falls. I retrieved the other half of the Sword, and have both pieces of the weapon in my skin."

"Celio!"

I turned to see Nevaeh running toward me.

She hugged me just like her brother did.

Beacon filled Navaeh in on everything, and his sister nodded after Beacon had finished talking.

"Okay," Nevaeh said, nodding. "Now all you need is my brother melding the Sword together, correct?"

I nodded. Yes."

"Well then, follow us," she responded, beckoning me with her hand.

"Yes, Celio. Follow us and I will meld both pieces of the enchanted weapon together," Beacon said.

I sighed before following the Archangel siblings, and as I did so, I touched my chest with my palm.

I had no idea how everything was going to go.

This was going to be interesting.

Beacon and Nevaeh led me to the Divine Castle, and all three of us entered.

We walked until we reached an empty room at the back of the castle.

The chamber was beautiful, with dark red curtains, and a vibrant patterned carpet.

Beacon, Nevaeh, and I entered before Beacon shut the door.

Then he turned to me.

"Okay, Celio. I need both pieces of the Sword so I can put them together."

I inhaled quickly, and then exhaled, taking off my shirt in order to retrieve the Empyrean Blade, as well as the portion that I found in the Heavenly Falls.

They both were solid tattoos, and I glanced down at my flesh, bringing my hand up to scrape my fingernails along my skin.

Within moments, I was able to grasp the handle of the separated weapons, pulling them both from my chest.

Beacon held out his hand as I grabbed the handles of the sharp objects, one after another. I gave them to him before I scratched my flesh once more.

The Empyrean Blade was then in my palms, and I handed that to Beacon. Soon after, I gave him the other piece.

He placed both portions of the Utopian Sword on a nearby table, arranging them so they would easily fit together.

Nevaeh and I watched as Beacon closed his eyes, reciting an incantation as he touched the fragments of the Sword.

A bright, white light engulfed the portions of the weapon.

The illumination was almost blinding, as it radiated from the sharp pieces. It receded within moments.

When Beacon peered down at the weapon, it was no longer in two fragments. It was whole.

I smiled as the Archangel turned toward me.

Then he spoke.

"And now, Acanthus and the Minotaur can be defeated."

Beacon brought the newly melded Utopian Sword to me, grabbing it by the handle, and put it in my palm.

"Put this in your chest and find Chrysanthe. Together, you both will be able to save the Realms," he said, watching my face carefully to make sure I was grasping what he was saying.

I nodded.

"Okay, Beacon. Alright."

71

My thick black wings emerged as I walked out of the Divine Castle, the newly forged Utopian Sword in my flesh.

I walked outside, looking around, trying to locate Chrysanthe.

I knew she'd been here, but after a while of searching, my eyebrows furrowed in confusion.

Where was Chrysanthe?

Where was she? Where was she? Where was she?

"Celio?"

I turned around at the sound of my name.

It was Serenity.

"Celio, are you looking for Chrysanthe?" she asked.

I nodded.

"She is back on Earth. Her scarred arm almost caused her to burn up in the Everlasting Light. Beacon and Nevaeh brought her back there so she could heal. She's stable now, though," Serenity quickly said, seeing my terrified face.

Chrysanthe almost burned up...

My heart pummeled my ribs in a panic.

"Thank you, Serenity," I told her.

And my wings were out before anything else was said.

72

Chrysanthe

oosebumps covered my skin as I stood by the window; the breeze was cold. I was watching the ink-black sky, the moon that was so beautiful...

I sighed, gazing at the stars, when there was a brush against my right arm. The sensation was accompanied by breath on my neck, my hair... I shut my eyes at the feeling, and I sensed arms wrapping around me.

"Are you feeling better?" Celio whispered as he pulled my body toward him.

My back was touching his chest as he ran his fingertips along my right arm. It sent a tingle through my system, from my head to my feet.

Although, I winced when he moved his fingers along the scarred portion of my arm.

"I'm sorry," Celio said, noticing how my body had tightened up at the touch.

It still stung, the scar, even though I'd had it for a while now. I was just going to have to deal with it.

But I did feel a lot better than I felt before.

The scar was just an ache as Celio touched it.

I heard and felt Celio sigh as soon as my body locked up. His breath hit the crook of my neck, saturating my skin, and running through my hair.

"I'm sorry," he repeated as he drenched me with warmth.

The more Celio talked, the more I could feel his oxygen on my neck.

"Don't be," I told him softly.

His breath continued to hit my shoulder. Then it traveled to my hair and my right ear.

I felt Celio's hand on my abdomen, holding me close to him. I could feel his palm on my abdomen, his breath on my neck, and his pulse against my skin.

Celio, I thought as I got soaked in oxygen from him.

I loved him so much…

I couldn't help it as his sweet-smelling breath hit my neck; I tilted my head to my left side as Celio brushed my blond hair away from my right shoulder.

The movement sent a jolt through my body.

I exhaled just as he whispered again.

"Chrysanthe," he said into my ear, and then I felt his lips on my shoulder, trailing all the way to the nape of my neck.

Heat rushed into my veins as I sighed at the sensation.

Celio paused as I twisted around to face him, his steady stare, his hazel eyes.

I felt his hand leave my abdomen, going to his side. I met his gaze, and then leaned forward, bringing my lips to his.

I brought my hands up, running my fingers through his hair as he kissed me back.

Celio…

He broke away from me after a few moments, gazing into my eyes again.

"I thought I was going to lose you," he said softly. "I thought… thought…"

Celio trailed off, not able to finish.

But I just put a finger to his lips, stopping him.

"I'm here now," I said.

"Chrys… Chrysanthe," Celio said again; I stopped him with a kiss.

"Shh," I said softly. "Shh," I repeated, breathing into his lips.

I kissed him again, but as soon as I pulled away, I wanted more. I abruptly craved Celio's touch. I wanted to comfort him.

I broke away, panting slightly.

It suddenly felt incredibly warm in the treehouse that we were in, even though it was nighttime.

One hand had a fistful of Celio's clothing, while my right dove into his short brown hair.

Celio groaned as I tried to get as close as possible to him.

The noise skittered along my bones, making my insides liquid.

That was when I felt his right hand meet the small of my back; we were so close together that I could feel his pulse. His quickening pulse.

Celio…

I loved him with all my heart.

My hand was still a fist as I held onto Celio's shirt. I just didn't want to let him go.

Celio.

His breathing was quick as he pulled away. His eyes were suddenly grasping mine in a way I'd never seen.

"Chrysanthe," he whispered into my mouth. "Chrysanthe, may I?"

I backed away so that I could see his expression, his hazel eyes that were burning into me. Into the essence of me.

"Yes," I breathed.

Celio blinked as he took my head in his hands, brushing my cheeks with his fingertips while he kissed me.

The sensation made my body liquid. My legs felt like they would give out.

I felt his palm slowly trace down my ribcage, all the way to my thighs. I shuddered, gazing at Celio as my body tingled.

He reached the bottom of my dress and slowly pulled it up, exposing my undergarments.

Every part of me was alert as Celio gently brought my dress up to my chest; I raised my hands over my head to help him.

I winced slightly as the fabric hit my scarred arm; Celio caught the expression as he tossed my dress to the side.

He gingerly grasped my right arm, bringing his lips to it. Then he pulled me close, kissing the crook of my neck again.

I inhaled slowly at the feeling, closing my eyes as my body suddenly felt like lightning had struck. A moan escaped my throat as I opened my eyes, seeing him look at me with his hazel ones.

Celio, I thought. *Celio…*

I brought my mouth to his as I ran my hands over his shirt, feeling his heartbeat underneath.

Celio just stayed still as I touched him.

My extremities trailed down his chest, to his abdominal muscles, to his hips. Then I went underneath his shirt, feeling his defined body.

Another groan escaped Celio as I felt the bottom of his clothing. He immediately brought his arms above his head, helping me take it off.

I couldn't help but marvel at his physique as I threw the garment to the ground.

My hands roamed across his flesh, and it was a few moments later, my fingertips hit the rough scar over his torso.

I inhaled quickly as I felt it, and then realized it was the scar from the Empyrean Blade, before Thana had been defeated.

She had stabbed Celio with the Blade, leaving him to bleed and die…

Tears began to form inside my eyes at the thought.

The thought of losing him…

I met Celio's eyes that were glued to mine, and then I brought my hands to the long scar.

Celio shut his eyes as I touched it. The scar went from the bottom of his ribcage to the middle of his abdomen. I felt him shiver as he put his head down.

I placed my hands on either side of the mark, and when Celio looked up again, I saw him stare, his eyes burning into the essence of me.

"Chrysanthe," he said softly, not breaking his gaze. "Chrysanthe," he repeated, pulling me close.

He kissed me as his hands grazed across my bare skin, from my shoulders to my hips.

My eyes fluttered, and I sighed softly.

Celio's hands were on my midriff, the sensation burning through my skin to my bones.

I settled my palms on his chest; I felt his pounding heart…

Gently, I pushed Celio toward the middle of the room. He continued to stare; he knew what I was doing, I could see it in his eyes.

His eyes that were burning into me.

"Celio," I murmured into his mouth.

He kissed me in response and then brought his lips to my neck.

I closed my eyes, welcoming the feeling, and a moan made its way through my throat.

Celio's hands grazed my body, and goosebumps erupted on my flesh.

I loved him. I loved him so much…

We reached the bed in the middle of the room, and that was when Celio gathered me up in his arms.

I kissed his neck, my heart pounding. My pulse was in my head, every bit of my body on alert as Celio whispered my name in my ear.

I sighed softly as he pulled me close…

Both of us were sweat-soaked, but I didn't care as my hands went down Celio's abdomen.

He groaned, and the noise tugged on my sanity.

I loved him.

I kissed him, and his lips found my throat, trailing to my right shoulder blade. My insides were liquid as our breath got intertwined, and my entire system was on fire as his hands roamed.

That was when our clothing all wound up on the ground, and I kissed Celio as we made it to the bed.

His body was so warm as he held me close…

The feeling erupted all over me; I couldn't get enough of him. The sensation burned through me, all over my body.

My mouth met Celio's once more as his back went on the bedsheets, and he groaned as my hands slowly trailed down his abdominal muscles.

I gently positioned myself on top of him, and the sound that came out of his throat made my body feel like it was on fire.

My entire system was alert as I watched my love close his eyes, before opening them again.

His hazel eyes burned through mine, grabbing the essence of me.

Celio stared at me for a split moment before he brought his left hand to my right cheek, grasping it softly as his mouth met mine.

He breathed into my lips as we broke apart slightly.

He watched me steadily as I moved, so my hips were right on top of his, running my palms along his bare chest.

I saw Celio's eyes flutter, and when he looked at me again, a powerful gaze took over his face.

It made my heart pulverize my ribs, and when I kissed him, I felt my long blond hair cascade around Celio's face.

"Chrysanthe," he breathed as my palms went to his neck, and my lips met his cheek.

Just the sound of him whispering my name sent a jolt of lightning through my veins.

The sensation stayed for what seemed like an eternity.

73

My eyes opened to the early morning sunlight through the treehouse window.

I squinted at the illumination, when I heard a sigh resound behind me.

The noise caused my heartrate to quicken.

My insides felt like liquid as I felt an arm wrap around my waist, a voice in my ear.

"Good morning, Chrysanthe," Celio said as he kissed the crook of my neck, causing me to close my eyes.

I welcomed the sensation and I touched Celio's hand on my abdomen.

I glanced down at my right hand before I moved in the bed, onto my back as I brought my left chrysanthemum-tattooed hand up to Celio's hair.

My fingers dove into his brown hair as I brought my lips to his, and I slowly brought myself upright.

I was on top of Celio, and I could feel my heart beating wildly as we broke away from one another.

He watched me silently, and his gaze began burning through me.

A groan shook through his throat as I ran my hands over his bare chest.

He shut his eyes as I put my hand over his heart, and I leaned forward and kissed him. My hands went from his heart to his neck.

I brought both of my palms to my love's neck, before I cupped his head in my hands, running my fingertips over his chin.

As I backed away, he was staring at me with a look in his eyes that I'd never seen before.

My eyelashes fluttered, and then he gently brought my face to his so that his mouth met mine.

The sensation was equivalent to a jolt of fire in my arteries.

As he pulled away, he was murmuring into my mouth.

"Chrysanthe," he whispered. "May I?"

His hands traveled up my figure as he spoke gently, causing tingles to rattle my spine.

I nodded, closing my eyes at the sensation before I spoke.

"Yes," I told him.

His lips met mine as he ran his palms over my bare skin, and my entire body felt like it was blazing.

Blazing for a while.

My entire body tingled as I put the straps of my undergarments and my dress back on, my heart pounding against my ribcage in the process.

A smile made its way on my face as I turned around and saw Celio, who was still in the bed.

He was just staring at me, and when our eyes met, his expression was so intense. It was like hunger mixed with awe.

I'd never seen that look on his face before last night or this morning.

So, this was a whole new feeling that I was experiencing.

The sensation cut into my bones and soaked into my bloodstream, and I continued to see Celio watching me.

His eyes were on mine for a few more moments before he finally got out of bed, putting his clothing on.

He walked over, gently grasping my head in his hands, and kissed me.

It was several moments before he pulled away.

"Chrysanthe, I love you."

"I love you too, Celio," I said after I recovered from the melting sensation I felt.

Celio and I smiled at each other, and then I heard a feral, guttural rumble resonate from outside.

I looked outside the treehouse window, only to see Caliya watching something.

The tigress was standing in the grass, her tail twitching as she focused on the atmosphere.

I followed Caliya's line of sight, but I couldn't really see anything.

It wasn't long before I heard a familiar screech in the early morning air.

I blinked as I saw a barn owl come into view, and I heard Celio come up behind me.

We both watched as Sybella's barn owl form flew toward the treehouse, getting closer and closer before Celio and I both backed up, allowing her to fly through the window.

She did so, and perched right on a nearby chair.

She clacked her beak for a bit, looked at us, and then took off, flying to the other side of the treehouse.

The blinding bright light engulfed her, before she transformed into her Being self.

Then she turned around, looking at both Celio and I.

"I heard about what happened, Chrysanthe," she said. "How is your arm feeling?" she then asked, watching me as I brought my extremity to my hair, tucking a piece behind my ear.

I saw Sybella focus on it, and then she brought her eyes back to mine.

"I need to recite the incantation again, so you don't have any more close calls."

Sybella walked over to me, and I extended my right extremity out, watching her silently as she put her palm on my arm and closed her eyes.

She recited the incantation, and opened her eyes when she was done.

"Now, you will be able to go back to the Afterworld. You are protected once more, Chrysanthe."

I felt Celio come up to my right side, grasping my hand in both of his.

"You are safe now, Chrysanthe," the Oracle said. "You are safe."

74

Acanthus

I was furious.

I was in the cave with the Minotaur, and it was nighttime.

I was seething as I glanced over at the bull-like creature, and I felt like my head was about to explode from the anger that was building inside me.

I punched the cave wall, trembling since I was so upset, but just let my back slide down to the ground.

I sank to the floor of the cave.

My heart was pounding so hard, I felt my pulse in my head.

I began to think back to what happened earlier, after the Oracle flew away in her bird form, but that just made me upset once more.

I was livid, but I still had the memory in my head of what I did after Sybella had flown away...

I shifted into a crow, flying over to see the Seer Sisters so that I could talk to them once more.

Although, when I got there, I was furious beyond belief.

I transformed back into my Being self after I landed in the swamp, and called out to Levana and Morana, who I knew were both inside the tent.

Levana poked her head out, the animal skull headpiece on so she could see clearly.

She came out of the tent, looking skeptical as to why I was there.

My heart was still pounding fiercely, my pulse still beating in my head.

But I tried to keep myself as calm as possible as I spoke to Levana.

As soon as the Seer Sister advanced toward me, I saw an ink black cat appear from the tent.

I saw the feline and squinted before I turned my attention back to Levana, who still looked nervous.

"What is it, Acanthus?" she asked. "What has happened now?"

I took a breath before I spoke.

"Two creatures have escaped from my grasp," I told her. "The Aureate Doe, as well as Sybella. Both of them have escaped after you told me their blood could open the entranceway to Hell."

I stopped, feeling fire in my head, but then I just swallowed back the bile that I sensed was rising in my throat.

Levana watched me for a few moments before she spoke.

She took a few steps closer to me as she did so.

"Acanthus, the only way to unlock the gateway to Hell is to destroy a Being or an animal whose blood is pure, and one that is not. The combined blood will then unlock the Inferno River, so that you can finally see Thana."

I glared at Levana, my eyes becoming slits.

I had already tried doing that with the pure Beings.

But I paused at what the Seer Sister had just told me.

Levana was an easy target.

A malicious smile took over my face, and I could see Levana's expression change as she saw the switch in my mood.

She took several steps back, but it was too late.

I took the enchanted skull from Levana, who began to scream as her eyes immediately turned milky- white and clouded.

Levana, as well as her sister Morana, were both now blind.

A meow caught my attention and I crouched to my knees, ready to pet the feline.

But Levana's milky white eyes grew wide as screams ripped from her lungs.

"No. No, please, don't hurt Melinoe! Don't hurt her! Please!"

I smiled sadistically.

I had the upper hand.

Now, Levana and Morana had to listen to ME.

I seethed.

Now, I had total control over the Seer Sisters.

I picked up Melinoe as Levana continued to plead, but it was no use.

I wasn't going to listen to her.

Wait.

I changed my mind.

No, I just had one question.

I glanced over at Levana, who, now in her blinded state, was getting more and more panicked.

That was when I spoke.

"Levana, where is Chrysanthe? Where is she right now?"

The Seer quickly responded.

"She is on Earth currently, but she is going to go to the Afterworld with her Archangel lover soon, along with Phoenix."

Levana shook after she spoke, and opened her mouth to talk once more, but I cut her off.

"Why was Chrysanthe on Earth? Was there a reason? Besides her being the Protector of it, why is she there?"

The Seer looked right at me with her white, blinded eyes. When she talked, her voice quivered slightly.

"Chrysanthe almost died. She almost burned up in the Everlasting Light that surrounds the Afterworld. The Oracle protected her with an incantation so that she could go to the Heavens without being harmed, since last time when Thana got defeated, Chrysanthe got scarred."

She took a breath before continuing.

"Since she was scarred by the Queen of the Underworld, Chrysanthe is unable to go to the Afterworld without an incantation to protect her. The spell was wearing off though, that is why Chrysanthe is on Earth."

Levana took a breath, and spoke once more.

But I didn't hear her.

Instead, I was thinking about Chrysanthe.

Just hearing about Chrysanthe almost dying made me shake in anticipation.

Chrysanthe could be hurt. Chrysanthe could be killed.

Chrysanthe could be killed.

But, as I knew, everything would come at a price.

Chrysanthe could burn up in the Everlasting Light that surrounded the Afterworld, and, unfortunately, I could as well, without the spell that I put on myself, in order to protect me when I traveled to the Afterworld and the Ethereal City.

But still, Chrysanthe could be harmed.

I looked straight at Levana, who was staring at me with her blind eyes, and noticed that Morana was poking her head out of the tent.

Morana was grabbing onto numerous objects blindly, attempting to find something sturdy to hold onto as she came outside.

Levana began talking again, pleading with me once more.

"Please, Acanthus. Please, let Melinoe go."

But I just stared at Levana, before shaking my head.

"No, I'm going to keep her. Once I find Chrysanthe and slaughter her, you can have your precious Melinoe. The only thing is, you're going to have to find her in the Abyss. She seems to really like me, so I'll bring her to Hell."

I held the enchanted skull headpiece in one hand, while Melinoe leaped onto my shoulder as I crouched down to pet her.

I closed my eyes afterward, felt fake Archangel wings erupt from my back, and flew off without another word.

Levana and Morana's screams echoed throughout the swampy marsh, but I ignored the noises.

Now, they were helpless.

I shook my head, returning to the present.

I glanced over to my right side, and saw the Minotaur, who was staring at me with his blood-red eyes.

I saw the Beast look over at the black cat named Melinoe, who was by my side.

"No. NO," I said forcefully at the Beast, who took one look at me before walking out of the cave.

The Minotaur left, heading outside in the forest to go hunt under the cover of darkness.

I watched the creature leave, before I saw the enchanted animal headpiece that once belonged to the Seer Sisters.

I smiled a sick smile before picking it up, fiddling with it aimlessly as my thoughts drifted to Chrysanthe, and how I was going to destroy her.

Destroy her, and then finally be reunited with Thana in Hell.

My fingers felt the headpiece as my thoughts ran wild in my head.

But I suddenly had an idea.

If the Seer Sisters could see with the headpiece, as well as view the future, could I see the future as well?

I squinted, thinking, before I put the headpiece on.

After I positioned the enchanted skull, I inhaled sharply.

I wasn't prepared for what happened next.

75

I gasped as I put the enchanted skull on my head.

I felt my eyes roll as I did so.

But as soon as I put the headpiece on, it was as if there were images cycling on repeat inside my brain.

Images that were important, significant, especially since I was trying to get back to Hell, to see Thana...

Image after image played in my mind.

An image of a stag with gigantic antlers. An image of a black-haired, tattooed Being who had various imprints on her skin.

Of deer skulls. Of spiders. Of snakes. Of crows.

An image of the Being holding the headpiece that was on my skull; she was putting a spell on it so that it was enchanted.

An image of the Seer Sisters, with Morana wearing the headpiece, while Levana stood next to her sibling, clutching her shoulder blindly.

She was speaking to someone else, a Being that had long, ink black hair that went to her elbows, even though it was held together in a huge, thick braid.

The other Being had a gigantic Fate Tattoo covering her heart. It was of the moon. She also had owl feathers on the outside of both of her hands.

The moon tattoo poked out through the top of the dress the Being was wearing, and even though it was a dark color, it worked for her.

The appearance was flattering.

The two female Beings were talking to each other, and then at one point the Being with the moon tattoo shrank instantly.

She became small in just a blink of an eye.

The Being turned... into a black cat.

A black cat with wide, blazing, yellow eyes.

The same cat that, actually, was right beside me.

The other Being, whose name I realized was Corvina, spoke to the feline, knowing that even though the Being was in disguise, she could still understand what was being told to her.

Corvina looked straight at the cat, speaking to her as if she was still in her Being form.

"And now, Layla, you will give me information about the Seer Sisters. Come back to me every time there is important news, and I will change you back into your Being form so you will have the ability to speak to me. For now, though, you are going to stay with the Seer Sisters."

I froze as the image dissolved.

It was several moments later that I grasped the headpiece with both hands, slowly taking it off.

I was speechless.

The black cat beside me, whose real name was Layla, had been given to the Seer Sisters by Corvina, a sorceress who had also given them the skull headpiece so that the siblings could see.

Not only that, but the cat was really a Celestial Being in disguise, and who was given to the Sisters so that Corvina could spy on them.

Which meant that Layla, known as Melinoe to Levana and Morana, had a lot of information about the Seer Sisters.

Maybe even more information about Chrysanthe.

I blinked, looking down at Layla as she watched me in her feline form, her yellow eyes blazing.

I carefully put the enchanted animal skull down on the floor of the cave, before turning my attention back to Layla.

She jumped first on my leg, and then on my left shoulder, positioning herself carefully. Then she draped her cat body around my neck so that two of her legs were on one side, and then two were on the other.

My eyebrows raised slightly as I felt the feline's body rise and fall as she breathed.

But then, an idea popped instantly into my head.

I needed to know exactly where Chrysanthe was.

I needed to know if she was still on Earth, or if she'd moved on to another Realm, or Realms, with her Archangel lover.

If so, I had to repeat the incantation I'd once stolen from a pure Celestial Being. Stolen from him before he died.

I'd also used his blood to go across the Realms; Thana had done the exact same thing in order to get out of Hell.

But, in order to track down Chrysanthe and cross the Realms, I would have to go to the sorceress who had turned Layla, the black cat currently on my neck, into a feline.

I would have to meet Corvina, say the incantation, and then find Chrysanthe and destroy her.

It all was a lot to do, but I was up for it.

But, first things first, I had to put on the headpiece to find out where Corvina was, where she lived.

Layla wouldn't be able to tell me anything in her cat form, so that was a job for the animal skull.

I picked up the enchanted headpiece, putting it on once more, before I had the sensation of my eyes rolling in the back of my head.

The images then surged through my brain, and I gritted my teeth as I viewed them.

It took a while to look through them all.

76

Chrysanthe

I looked at Sybella, her words directed at me, but I couldn't really soak them in.

I trembled as the memory of the agony of my right arm took over my brain.

And then I felt fingers graze across my extremity. I gulped.

I looked at Celio as he approached. He wrapped his arms around me, and I smiled as we locked eyes.

Then I brought my attention back to the Oracle.

"I'm sorry," I told her. "I'm just-"

"Scared," Sybella said.

I nodded. "Yes. Yes, I am."

"Well, now that the incantation has been said, and you are here on Earth, you are safe. As long as I am with you in the Afterworld, you are protected."

I nodded before watching Celio, who still had me in an embrace.

"Protected by both of us, you mean, Sybella?"

The Oracle smiled, looking at my love.

"Yes," she said, grinning. "Yes, Celio. Yes, of course."

I smiled along with Celio and Sybella, before I paused. My breathing stopped as I thought of something.

My dream.

My dream where I turned into Thana.

"Umm… umm…" I stuttered.

I got Sybella's attention as I struggled to speak.

"Yes?"

"I never told you about my dream, have I?"

Sybella shook her head. "No. No, you haven't, Chrysanthe. What was your dream about?"

I paused; the Oracle stiffened at my body language.

"I dreamt about Thana again. I had another dream that I had turned into Thana."

Sybella froze for a moment or two before she finally spoke.

"Like when you were staying with me," she said in almost a whisper. She swallowed, and then looked in my direction. "You were having the dream about Thana because the incantation to keep you safe wore off. That was why you were in so much pain as well. If you hadn't been rushed here to Earth by Nevaeh and Beacon, you would've died. Died, and gone to the Abyss, since you were- and are- scarred by the Queen of the Underworld."

I gulped, while I felt Celio's arms tighten around me.

"It's a good thing you were brought to Earth at the right moment," he said.

I locked eyes with Celio.

"Yes, that is a good thing. It's a good thing that Chrysanthe is safe," Sybella stated. "It's a very good thing."

Acanthus

emory after memory soared through my mind as I wore the headpiece.

An image of the Seer Sisters.

An image of a stag.

An image of the Inferno River.

Finally, I just commanded the headpiece to show me one image, Corvina.

The sorceress popped up in my brain, and then there was another image of a cottage.

A cottage in an overgrown, gloomy forest.

I grinned menacingly.

Now, I would be able to find Corvina, which also meant that I would finally be able to find Chrysanthe.

78

I finally found out where Corvina lived.

It wasn't that far away from where the Seer Sisters actually were, so I decided to morph into an Archangel and go to the swampy marsh.

After I went to the marsh, I could just go into the forest nearby, and to the cottage where Corvina lived.

A meow quickly interrupted my thoughts as Layla pushed her body against my leg.

I leaned down to pet her furry body before I paused and smiled maniacally.

I might as well just bring her with me, I thought.

I grasped Layla and then shifted so I had black wings erupt from my back.

Holding her close to my chest, I flew off, the thought of Corvina in my mind the entire trip.

79

I recognized Corvina's cottage as I landed in the swampy, insect-infested, marshy forest.

I landed and Layla started squirming, attempting to escape from my arms as soon as I landed on the smelly turf.

"Okay, Layla. Okay, just calm down," I said to the ink-black cat. "Here," I told her as I crouched down and let her jump out of my arms.

She bounded toward the cottage, looking behind her as she made her way through the uneven and damp terrain.

She was definitely a shape-shifter, or was a Being put under a spell to be an animal.

The way Layla was looking back at me was definitely a Being way instead of an instinctual way that would be feral, like a wild animal.

Layla kept looking behind her, until I finally followed her feline form.

She paused once she got to the cottage door, and when I reached it, I knocked twice.

Then I backed up, Layla meowing at the entranceway.

It was only a few minutes later that I saw the door open, and then... Corvina was there, looking at me cautiously.

She was cautious, as well as surprised.

"Hello," she said carefully. "How can I help you?"

Corvina paused, peering down at Layla, who now was walking around Corvina's feet.

She took one glance at Layla, before peering back up at me.

Understanding filled her face, and that was when she opened the door wide, allowing me to enter.

"Come on in, Acanthus. Come on in."

"You found me from the Seer Sisters' enchanted skull, didn't you?" Corvina asked, sitting down at a dark table in the middle of the dining area.

She sat across from me, and I nodded in response.

"Yes, I stole the headpiece from the Sisters since I wasn't succeeding in anything they were telling me. I was supposed to steal the Aureate Doe, capture Phoenix, and then find the Utopian Sword. But, I captured the Doe -only for it to escape- I haven't been able to find Phoenix- he is probably with Chrysanthe, plotting to destroy me- and lastly, I have to find the Utopian Sword. The weapon has been extremely difficult to look for."

My jaw clenched just thinking about everything.

How I was failing at finding, or keeping, the items.

I was livid about the whole thing.

I ground my teeth together.

"I have to find the items in order to kill Chrysanthe, and eventually be reunited with Thana."

That's all I ever wanted.

To be with Thana in Hell...

I shook my head, clearing it, but as I did so, I spotted Corvina looking straight at my arms.

She squinted.

"Acanthus. Acanthus, where are your Fate Tattoos?"

I saw her blink rapidly as she saw both of my bare arms.

She instantly appeared worried, but I just rolled my eyes.

Yet another thing to be blown out of proportion, the fact that I used my Fate Tattoos to terrorize the Ethereal City.

"What about my Fate Tattoos?" I asked in a drawl.

"Acanthus, if you let your Fate Tattoos out of your skin to wreak havoc, the only one you are wreaking havoc on is yourself. Phoenix, Chrysanthe, or Celio- any other powerful Celestial Being for that matter- will be able to hurt you by causing damage to your Fate Tattoo."

The sneer on my face quickly disappeared.

My eyes widened.

"Acanthus, that was how Thana became weakened. Weakened enough to be killed with the Empyrean Blade, and sent to the Abyss permanently." Corvina shook her head in sudden disbelief. "Perhaps Thana and you really *do* belong together," the Being muttered under her breath.

She said it in a whisper to herself, but I could still hear her.

Automatically, my lip curled up in disgust, and a growl erupted from my throat.

I snarled as I stood up from the table, looking at Corvina threateningly.

But Corvina just rolled her eyes as I stood to my full height.

Anger pulsed through my blood as I stared at her, but she wouldn't budge.

My hands curled into fists, and that was when, to my surprise, she stood up as well, glaring right at me.

Her blue eyes blazed into mine as she stared me down.

"Really, Acanthus? Do you really want to go up against me? I could turn you into a bug and kill you within only a few moments. Do you want to die today?"

My lip was still curled up in a snarl, but inside, I felt taken aback.

No one had ever gone up against me like that.

Never.

I'd always been the stronger one when it came to conflicts.

Corvina glared as she spoke again.

"Watch what you say to me, Acanthus, or I will make sure that you are separated permanently from your Queen of Hell."

I gritted my teeth as she spoke; I was positively livid.

But I couldn't- and didn't- say a word.

"Now, can we continue our conversation? Or are you going to lose your temper again?"

I stood, glaring at Corvina, but my hands went to my sides, my fists unfurling.

"We can talk now?"

I nodded, and then sat back down.

But inside, I was so angry.

I didn't have the power that I thought I had.

That fact made me extremely upset.

orvina took a deep breath in through her lungs as she sat back down, watching me dead in the eyes as I seethed.

It was as soon as my anger melted away that I saw Corvina's stare weaken.

But I still was stone-faced when she spoke.

"What I was trying to say before you lost your temper," Corvina started, "was that Thana was weakened when she had her crow Fate Tattoo out of her skin. Sybella, in her barn owl form, latched onto Thana's crow tattoo with her talons, and that was what made her weak enough to get killed by the Empyrean Blade, the Blade that Chrysanthe had. Thana was killed by Chrysanthe, getting banished to the Abyss once more."

I blinked for several moments, before looking at Corvina, who then looked down at Layla.

Corvina picked her up, staring at the cat thoughtfully, before she just looked the black feline dead in the eyes.

She held Layla with one hand, while with the other, she held out her palm and flicked her wrist around.

That one movement made Layla morph back into a Celestial Being.

A Being that was covered in a moon Fate Tattoo, along with owl feathers on the outside of each of her hands.

Layla, now a Celestial Being again, was watching me, and then Corvina was as well.

Corvina spoke up as Layla looked at me.

"Layla will be able to help you, Acanthus."

81

y eyebrows furrowed in confusion as I turned my attention to Layla.

"How is she going to help me?"

"She is going to help you because she has-"

"The Crescent Stone," Layla finished.

My expression stayed the same as I became bewildered.

I had never heard of that stone before.

"What will the Crescent Stone do? How is that going to help me?"

Layla was the one who answered.

"The Crescent Stone has the power to make anyone or anything fall asleep. Whether it be a Celestial Being, Archangel or animal. It also has the ability to manipulate dreams. I have the ability to control the moonlight, the tides, and the seasons."

Layla sighed.

"I used to use the Crescent Stone and my abilities for good, but my partner has been with so many female Beings- and even some mortals- now that I have given up on him."

Layla looked over to the side, breaking the eye contact that she had on me for a few moments before turning back.

"I will help you, Acanthus, as long as you agree to help me in return."

I squinted, wanting to know what she was going to say next.

"Come to the Aerial Alpines with me. Help me destroy Shadow."

I nodded, acknowledging Layla's words.

I could see Corvina watching the both of us out of the corner of my eye, staying silent.

"Okay, Layla," I said finally. "I'll do that for you. I'll help you and go to the Aerial Alpines."

"Thank you, Acanthus. I appreciate that. Now, let's go to the Ethereal City and get your Fate Tattoos returned to your skin."

We both looked at Corvina, before we left the cottage in the marshy, smelly forest that was beside the Inferno River and the Seer Sisters.

I morphed into an Archangel so I could have wings, and Layla transformed back into a cat.

I picked her up, holding her close to my chest as I flapped my wings.

And we both ascended into the atmosphere.

A wild, feral, guttural snort erupted from the ground as I held onto Layla; I knew automatically that the intimidating noise was the Minotaur.

He was still hunting, even in the daylight.

But, then again, the bull-like creature was consistently hungry.

He could eat anything at any moment.

The blood- curdling screeches rang in my ears as I landed, and Layla squirmed in my arms at the sound.

When I let her down on the ground, she instantly transformed into her Celestial Being body.

She looked at me with a disdainful expression.

The seething, angry emotion that Layla was giving me hurt as bad as me getting ripped open with a knife.

The shrieking in the distance continued for a few more moments, before there was a bone crunching, violent crack, and then the screeches stopped.

A savage, noisy crunch killed the silence as the Minotaur began to eat, and I looked at Layla as she continued to give me a disgruntled expression.

She got over it quickly though, instead walking ahead of me, walking toward the Ethereal City.

"Come on, Acanthus," Layla said. "Let's go get your Fate Tattoos back inside your skin, and then I'll be able to help you with the Crescent Stone."

Layla and I walked in silence.

We didn't say a word to each other as we walked through the forest, eventually getting to the outskirts of the woods and entering the Ethereal City.

But I saw and heard a bird scream, and I looked up to the sky, only to realize that flames were accompanying the creature.

I glared as it hit me, and a deep rumble erupted from the core of my body as I saw the animal.

Layla and I had been spotted.

Spotted by Phoenix.

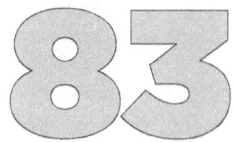

Chrysanthe

A bird flying toward the treehouse caught my attention as I looked outside.

I stared, before I realized that it was Phoenix.

His red-orange wings were flapping hard as he made his way to the window, and eventually flew through it.

Morphing quickly by bursting into flames, he turned back into his Being form, and looked at Celio and I.

He sounded out of breath as he spoke.

"Celio, Chrysanthe," he started, taking in a gulp of oxygen before continuing. "I just saw Acanthus and a female Celestial Being leaving the forest and entering the Ethereal City. The Minotaur is also there, the creature, it had been hunting throughout the night and early this morning."

My blood ran cold.

The Minotaur had been hunting.

Hunting Celestial Beings all night long and this morning…

Acanthus was there too, ready to cause panic and havoc in the place where pure, honorable Beings were supposed to live in harmony with others and the environment.

Phoenix glanced at Celio, and that was when his eyes zeroed in on the top of Celio's chest, where the handle of the Utopian Sword was poking out.

The Sword that was hidden in Celio's skin as a Fate Tattoo.

Phoenix talked after some silence.

"Celio, you have to give the Sword to Chrysanthe," he said, and I turned around and looked at Phoenix.

I knew I was the only one who would be able to kill Acanthus and the Minotaur.

It was so unnerving to me, though.

Even though it appeared that way, I still accepted the enchanted weapon as Celio took off his shirt, scraped his skin with his fingernails, and removed the Sword from his flesh.

My love handed it to me, and I took it gingerly, slowly but methodically pushing it into my skin, right over my heart until it appeared as a Fate Tattoo.

I took a half-glance at Phoenix, and then at my love.

Celio had an encouraging expression on his face, but it was also mixed with nervousness.

But he stopped the look from taking over his face, and then he smiled.

Phoenix talking was what made us look away from each other.

"We must all go to the Ethereal City. *Now*," Phoenix finished, an urgent tone to his voice.

He instantly burst into flames as he turned into the fiery bird, and then took off out of the treehouse.

Celio and I watched him leave, and that was when Celio looked at me, walking over.

A small smile was now on his face as he peered into my eyes with his hazel ones, and then I felt his palms around my waist.

He wrapped his arms around my body, and I felt my feet leave the ground as he positioned me in his arms.

I grinned, kissing his cheek before I saw his black wings erupt from his back. Within moments, we were airborne and headed to the Ethereal City.

84

Acanthus

I ground my teeth together, making my hands into fists, unfurling them, and then making a fist again.

My Fate Tattoos were back in my skin, and I could see, out of the corner of my eye, that Layla was watching me as we went back into the woods.

I was shaking; I was so upset.

In my peripheral vision I saw Layla turning toward me.

"You will help me, right? After I help you defeat and kill Chrysanthe?"

I was so livid, but I turned to her, nodding at her words as I stayed silent.

"Okay then. You better stay true to your word, though, because if you don't, I will easily put you into an eternal sleep. Either with the Crescent Stone, or with my abilities in general."

I turned to Layla, exposing my teeth to her.

"No. Don't," she said, stopping me. "Don't even start. You don't scare me."

I growled at Layla, but then backed off.

Yet again, I wasn't able to intimidate or threaten a Celestial Being.

I just looked at the ground as I made fists.

I was not used to being told the word, 'No.'

"You don't scare me, Acanthus," Layla said.

My upper lip curled in disgust at her, revealing a snarl.

"Don't do it," she uttered. "You keep doing that, and I will *not* help you. And, as I could say from the conversation I had with Corvina, you need my assistance to finally destroy Chrysanthe."

I inhaled, but then was glaring at Layla's words.

I exhaled in a gust, and continued clenching my fists, but stayed silent the entire rest of the way through the forest.

Layla and I walked in complete silence before she paused, peering around the wooded area.

She sensed something as she looked around, and that was when a bird screeched.

The loud noise carried throughout the marshy forest.

The piercing sound was followed by the sight of a fireball.

I gritted my teeth together as Layla was just watching silently.

Although, I could see out of my peripheral vision, that her arms were quivering the same way a cat would thrash its tail around whenever it would watch its prey.

Both Layla and I anticipated what would come next, as the fireball was seen again, and Phoenix flew straight toward us, ready to attack.

We watched as Phoenix headed our way, and I seethed, a sadistic smile taking over my face.

This was going to be fun.

Chrysanthe

elio's wings flew out in front of him as he landed in the Ethereal City with me in his arms.

As he let go of me though, we both heard a guttural, feral roar, and our eyes widened before we heard a bird scream.

Celio and I both ran to the edge of the forest, only to see the tail feathers of Phoenix in the Minotaur's mouth.

Phoenix was still in the fiery bird form, but he had flown to the branch of a nearby tree.

I gasped, but unfortunately, that was the wrong thing to do.

Acanthus, the Minotaur, and an unfamiliar female Being all looked in my direction.

That was when I stared at Thana's Beast, and gulped.

But the Minotaur took that as a cue to charge. He ran right at Celio and I, right in our direction.

86

The Minotaur rushed toward us, running full speed, but then there was a flash of fire, and then Phoenix was there.

His tail feathers regenerated since he was able to heal quickly.

Phoenix flew right into the Minotaur's face, in front of Celio and I, and I threw my hands up.

The Beast immediately retreated as Phoenix was in front of us.

Tree vines erupted from my hands as the bull-like creature bellowed; the vines and thorns hit the Minotaur square in the jaw.

It bellowed once more, in both agony and frustration, and that was when I heard a scream.

I looked past the bull-like animal, only to see Acanthus running toward me, appearing livid.

He quickly morphed into a gigantic black wolf as he ran at Phoenix, and leaped at him.

Phoenix fell straight to the ground as he was tackled by Acanthus' wolf body; I heard him scream in pain as he was pinned by Acanthus' canine paw.

But Phoenix wasn't pinned for long.

I opened my hands again, bringing my palm out and sending thorny vines right at Acanthus' face.

He yelped in pain as the thorns hit his muzzle, and that was when the female Celestial Being came out of the woods. She glanced at the Hell Being that was bleeding profusely from the thorns. That, and the Minotaur that had collapsed.

She glared at me, but Phoenix finally got loose from Acanthus' grip after he, in his wolf form, moved his paw.

Phoenix freed himself, and burst into flames right behind the female Being, who was oblivious to him.

She was just staring at me.

I looked at her, and she just smirked.

I was confused.

"Who are you?" I asked her, honestly wanting to know the truth.

I didn't understand what was going on.

But the female was silent, all while continuing to advance toward me, long enough for Celio to see the Crescent Stone in her hand.

The Crescent Stone could be used for good or evil, depending on who possessed it. The Archangels, as well as Celestial Beings, knew of its power and strength.

Being an Archangel, and also having the ability to manipulate and control dreams, Celio understood immediately what was going to happen next.

The female Being was going to use the Stone to put both Celio and I to sleep, so that we could be killed easily by Acanthus and the Minotaur.

Celio saw the sadistic grin on her face, and his eyes widened before he pulled me close in an embrace, bringing his wings out at full span. He wrapped them around me in a protective manner.

The wings wrapped all the way around me, so my body was completely covered, along with Celio's.

Celio and I could both hear the female Being laugh, and I knew by the way she sounded that she was amused. Amused by the way Celio was choosing to protect me.

She continued to laugh, before she spoke.

"Alright, then, you two. Say goodnight."

Acanthus

I stayed in my wolf form.

I was still in pain from the thorns Chrysanthe made in order to hinder me.

I whimpered in pain, but when I looked up from my paw, where I was also bleeding, I saw Layla holding the Crescent Stone right in front of her.

The clear stone was right in her palm before she blew the dust that was naturally on the jewel, right on Chrysanthe's lover.

Even though her lover's black wings were protecting Chrysanthe, the dust blew onto his wings, getting trapped in his feathers.

This all caused the Archangel to collapse moments after Layla used the Stone.

He fell away from Chrysanthe, falling to the ground with his Archangel Fate Tattoo wings exposed.

Chrysanthe's Archangel lover had been knocked unconscious.

Chrysanthe

My eyes widened as I saw Celio on the ground of the Ethereal City, knocked out by the unfamiliar female Celestial Being. When I looked up, she was laughing maniacally.

"Don't worry," the female said to me, in a tone that was a drawl. "Your lover is fine. He's just asleep."

I blinked, stunned.

"Who... who... are you?"

She smirked before she spoke.

"I'm the Celestial Being of Darkness."

My eyebrows furrowed. I had never heard of that.

The Being watched me, before she talked again.

"I'm the Queen of the Night."

I just stared at her, stunned, and then turned my attention toward Celio. Then, I inhaled.

The female Being was Queen of the Night.

She could control and manipulate dreams, the darkness, and sleep. She also had the ability to control the moonlight, the tides, and the seasons.

I looked at her, before seeing her moon Fate Tattoo that was poking out through the top of her dress.

Oh, I thought as I put it all together.

I immediately remembered a conversation between me and the Oracle.

It was about a Celestial Being named Layla, who had a love named Shadow.

Well, she loved him, but he was consistently cheating on her.

With mortals, as well as other Beings.

Layla loved Shadow, but after all the cheating, she had given up on love.

Now, she was ruthless to others.

I shook my head a bit, coming out of my reverie and back to the present.

Layla was just watching me, breathing heavily from all the anger stored up inside her.

She opened up her mouth to speak, and when she did, it was through her teeth.

"Now, Chrysanthe," she seethed. "I'm going to destroy you."

Layla glared at me, but then I straightened my back, and squinted as I looked at her.

I was my father's daughter.

Viro was part of my bloodline.

Which meant that I had the power to take control of the weather.

I suddenly felt fire in my veins as I brought both of my hands up, my palms toward the sky, and flicked both of my wrists quickly.

Thunder crackled throughout the atmosphere, making Layla jump.

She tried to retaliate instantly, but I flicked my wrist once more, and green vines appeared, right by Layla's bare feet.

The vines and the thorns soared up Layla's legs, heading toward her waist, and trapping her as the spiked plant curled around her chest.

She could still breathe, but she was trapped.

Now, she had nowhere to go.

89

Layla struggled against the plant restricting her, but the movement only made them tighten around her body.

I walked over to her as she continued to strain her muscles, but it was no use.

I saw the Crescent Stone in Layla's hand and took it. She then attempted to shift into an animal in order to get away.

She morphed into a black cat.

She became a feline, hissing at me, but I, having the ability to control and heal nature, stopped Layla in her cat form by flicking my wrist again as I focused on her.

I pulled Layla toward my body, all while the cat was hissing and yowling.

But I was unfazed.

I pulled her along with one hand, while I had the Crescent Stone in the other.

By that point, Layla was being extremely difficult.

She was hissing and smacking the air with her claws extended, but again, I was unfazed.

I just didn't want her to go anywhere. I couldn't have her run away.

But I could use the Stone against her.

Layla hissed, livid as could be, and that was when I finally held out the Crescent Stone, blowing the dust that was around it into her face.

Layla quickly became unconscious, even though she was the Queen of the Night.

She was knocked out immediately.

I took the Crescent Stone, and held it tightly in my hand, walking over to Celio, who was on the ground.

He was still unconscious, his wings completely out of his back.

I walked up to his sleeping frame, gently pushing a sweaty tendril of hair from his forehead, and then blew on the Crescent Stone once I put it near his face.

"Celio?" I asked gently. "Celio, wake up."

I kissed his cheek lightly, before I saw his eyes flutter open.

But right as I saw the loving gaze he gave me; I saw him look in the distance.

Panic was on his face.

A deep, feral, guttural sound was behind me.

I turned, only to see the ink-black Minotaur charging toward both Celio and I.

Again.

Instantly, I grasped my heart, quickly scraping my fingernails over my skin and pulling the Utopian Sword out of my flesh.

It was only a moment later that the Minotaur was in front of me, getting ready to gore me with its horns.

A deep bellow escaped from its lungs as it charged, but I ducked at the right moment.

I missed being harmed by inches.

I threw the sharp edge of the enchanted weapon around as I moved, but I hit the Minotaur's horns.

This just enraged the beast further; it let out a loud rumble.

It shook through the Minotaur's dark black muzzle as the creature twisted its body around.

It stared at me with blood-red eyes before I saw a gargantuan vulture flying toward me with frightening speed.

It was just about to attack me when Phoenix burst into view, seemingly out of nowhere, setting fire to the vulture with his flaming feathers.

The predatory bird screamed in pain, backing off immediately, but that was when I saw the vulture shudder, instantly changing into different creatures as the flames burned.

The animal shifted some more, before it crashed to the ground in noticeable agony.

My eyebrows furrowed in confusion, but that was when I saw the animalistic shapeshifter turn back into his Being form.

My eyes widened as I saw his short black hair, his green eyes when he opened them, and looked directly at me.

That was when I realized who the Being was.

It was Acanthus.

It was Acanthus.

It was Acanthus.

The Being from Hell that had caused such destruction was right in front of me.

I gulped as he opened his green eyes. He stared straight at me.

His lip curled upward, and he seethed when he saw me.

The disgusted expression burned and bored into my chest.

Bored into my heart.

His teeth were gritted so hard I thought his head was going to explode.

Acanthus was just so angry...

I stepped backward, feeling the animosity radiating off the Hell Being.

The Utopian Sword was still in my hand, my palm still on the handle in a vice-like grip.

I held the Sword tightly as Acanthus continued to glare at me.

I sensed Celio behind me, getting upset, but it was *my job* to destroy Acanthus and the Minotaur.

I was the only Being that would be able to go up against both of them.

90

I followed Acanthus' eyes with my own as he glared at me. I took a deep breath as we watched each other, but then I heard the bellow behind me.

I turned at the right moment, jumping out of the path of the Minotaur before he could gore me.

But that was my mistake.

My mistake as Acanthus was now behind me, attempting to charge, but Celio protected me as my back was turned.

I felt Celio's wings brush my cheek as I faced the Minotaur, all while the creature was staring me down with blood-red eyes.

It then ran toward me, but I hit the Minotaur's body with the Utopian Sword.

The weapon grazed the side of the Minotaur before it could harm me with its horns.

A loud, agonizing cry escaped from its throat as it partially leaped backwards in pain, and I heard Acanthus scream.

Anger ripped through him as I twisted my body around, and I saw Acanthus run straight at me, looking like he was ready to slam me to the ground.

Celio tried to protect me, staying in front of me, but Acanthus shifted into a vulture fast. It happened in the span of a heartbeat.

Acanthus jumped into the air, shifting into a massive vulture, dodging Celio before trying to attack me.

But I was faster.

I gripped the handle of the Utopian Sword tightly, before bringing it up above my head in one swift motion, slicing through the air with the weapon.

I hit Acanthus' shapeshifted form.

He screeched in agony as he fell, and crashed to the ground.

Acanthus was bleeding profusely as I looked at him. But then he began morphing again. Morphing into various animals, Beings, and Archangels.

I squinted in confusion, but only for a moment.

It was after that that I remembered something.

Thana.

It was about Thana.

About how when she died, she had started to shift into who she really was.

I blinked when I realized that that was what was going on with Acanthus.

I sighed as I watched him get weaker and weaker, bleeding heavily.

But then I saw him take his few final breaths, and saw his body deteriorate into black dust.

Black dust which then floated through the air and high into the atmosphere.

91

The blood pooling on the ground of the Ethereal City was the only remnant of Acanthus.

That was all that was left of the Hell Being.

A deafening roar ripped through the air, and I knew before I twisted around that it was the Minotaur.

I immediately knew that the bull-like creature had seen Acanthus die.

I heard hooves pound against the ground, and realized that the Minotaur was preparing to tear me apart.

I brought the Utopian Sword up over my head, bringing it down in one swift motion as the Beast came scarily close to me.

I hit the Minotaur right in the left shoulder, causing it to stagger backwards.

It staggered, and then a rumble deep within its chest ripped through its lungs.

A rumble of agony.

Blood began to pour from the wound, and right as it staggered back, Phoenix, in his bird form, flew past me, crossing in front of the Minotaur.

Phoenix set everything around the creature on fire.

But the flames surrounding the bull-like beast were short-lived as the Minotaur stomped through them roughly.

It quickly put out the fire that was in its way, running toward me and giving me a look of ferocity that was both scary and intimidating. It made my heart skip a beat.

My blood pulsed in my head as I pushed past the fear that I felt swimming in my veins, and I gripped the handle of the now bloodied Utopian Sword.

I breathed rapidly, while the sensation of fear, adrenaline, and anger entered my system.

I glared at the Minotaur, holding the enchanted weapon before angling the Sword, and stabbing the creature right in the chest.

A terrifyingly intimidating grunt mixed with a cry of agony blistered through the Minotaur, and blood poured out not only from the shoulder wound, but from the chest injury as well.

The noise which had radiated from the creature's throat just a short while ago changed instantly into a wheezing, disconnected pant.

Then the Minotaur stopped breathing, slumping over and doing a faceplant into the ground of the Ethereal City.

That was when it happened, the final breath of the Beast.

And then…

The Minotaur was dead.

92

hoenix flew up to Celio and I, morphing back into his Being self before looking down at the Utopian Sword in my hand.

The weapon was covered in blood.

Phoenix was looking at the Sword, and then he brought his eyes to mine.

"Chrysanthe," he started, "the blood of the Minotaur and Acanthus mixed with the blood of you," he looked at me, "and Celio," he looked at my love, "will unlock the Water of the Heavenly Falls."

Phoenix glanced at Celio and I, before he spoke again.

He brought his attention to our extremities.

"Hold out your palms," he instructed, looking at us.

We exchanged glances for a moment, before we did what we were told.

We both put our palms out in front of us, and then Phoenix pulled a sharp blade out of the pocket of his shorts.

He had the sharp weapon in one hand, while he had a cloth in the other.

Quickly, he sliced through the skin of my hand, causing me to wince, but the pain subsided as he took a special potion from his shorts.

He doused my palm, and then covered the wound with a cloth.

A few droplets of blood escaped, but Phoenix had a vial so that he could capture it.

Phoenix repeated the same thing with Celio.

Once he was done, Phoenix leaned forward as I grasped the Utopian Sword.

He took a bit of the blood on the weapon; he had the blood of Celio and I, mixed with the blood of both Acanthus and the Minotaur.

Phoenix looked at Celio and I.

Then he spoke.

"Now, with the blood of both of you, mixed with the blood of the enemies that were threatening the Afterworld and the Ethereal City, you two can save each other. Save each other, as well as Viro and Thera. Here, Chrysanthe," Phoenix said, giving me the vial of red bodily fluid. "Go to the Heavenly Falls, and tell Hali what happened. After that, give this to her."

Phoenix smiled.

"You saved everyone, Chrysanthe."

Phoenix's hair began to smoke slightly, and then he burst into a fireball, transforming into his bird form and flying away without another word.

93

I watched Phoenix leave in silence, watching him as he flew through the atmosphere.

Feeling Celio's arms around my body made all the tension in my body automatically disappear. He kissed my shoulder blade.

"You did it, Chrysanthe. You destroyed the enemy, and saved the Realms," he said, holding me close.

I smiled, and then brought my attention to my surroundings.

There was no longer a dreary sensation around the Ethereal City.

It was very rewarding.

I took a deep inhale through my lungs, exhaling as I realized that the Ethereal City and the Afterworld were both safe.

Actually, *all* the Realms were now safe.

I felt my heartrate become even as I looked around, seeing everything around me appear healthy, natural.

The way the Ethereal City was supposed to appear.

I finally felt relaxed, and I smiled. The expression left my face momentarily though, when there was a bleating noise behind me.

My eyebrows furrowed in confusion, but then I remembered the Doe.

The Aureate Doe.

She was here.

Twisting my body around, that was exactly what I saw.

I inhaled quickly as I thought about Cyra.

She must've been worried sick about her.

And then there was the promise that I had made to the Celestial Being, that I would bring the Doe back to her.

I had to go back to the Aerial Alpines, and bring the Aureate Doe back to Cyra.

I turned my head to glance at Celio, who was watching me carefully.

"You want to bring her back to Cyra, don't you?" he asked softly.

Celio was always able to sense what I was thinking, even though he wasn't able to read minds.

I smiled, before bringing my attention back to the Doe, who was now walking up to me carefully, sniffing my hand.

A soft laugh exited my throat as the Doe licked my extremity, and I knew after that that the Aureate Doe trusted me.

Trusted me enough to pick her up. I cradled her in my arms carefully.

I heard Celio whistle as I turned around, and that was when I heard and saw the black Winged Horse come into view.

He whinnied as he threw his wings back, landing on the ground of the Ethereal City.

My hands were full as I looked at Maximus, but that was when Celio walked up to me.

"Put the Doe down, Chrysanthe," he said. "Put her down and get on Maximus. I'll bring her to Cyra."

I nodded.

That made more sense.

I put the Aureate Doe on the ground, and I heard Maximus nicker affectionately.

I put my hand on his head, in between his ears, and played with the bit of his mane that was between his eyes.

I rubbed his ears as he moaned gently.

I smiled, looking at Celio's face, and he was also smiling.

Maximus had a rumble come out of his chest, and as I looked again at the Winged Horse, he bowed, allowing me to get on him.

"Chrysanthe," Celio said, making me look at him from the tone of his voice. He was right next to me. He kissed my cheek. "I'll be right behind you with the Aureate Doe," he said as he backed away. "I'll be with you."

I was right in thinking that Cyra would be happy getting the Aureate Doe back.

When Maximus landed in the Aerial Alpines with me on his back, she appeared hopeful, but once she saw Celio fly and land next to me with the Doe in his arms, Cyra was ecstatic.

The Aureate Doe appeared to have the same reaction, and Celio put her on the ground quickly so that she could bound over to Cyra, who was crying tears of happiness.

"Thank you," she said as she cried. "Thank you both so much."

94

Celio

I turned my attention to Chrysanthe as she watched Cyra, before looking back at me.

We locked eyes, and then I spoke.

"Can we go to the Heavens now, Chrysanthe?" I asked her softly. She nodded.

"Yes. Yes, we can."

I twisted my body around, seeing the black Winged stallion look at me with his brown eyes.

I walked forward, and he bowed low.

I had one hand on his head and one hand by my side as I looked at Chrysanthe, who was grinning.

She watched me steadily before glancing at Cyra.

"Bye, Cyra," Chrysanthe said, afterward turning and looking at me once more.

She then got on Maximus, so the Winged Horse was carrying both of us.

Maximus was going to bring us both to the Afterworld.

Chrysanthe climbed onto Maximus, and gripped his mane as I was behind her, making sure she wouldn't fall off.

She then clicked her tongue.

I saw the Winged Horse flap his enormous, thick, black appendages.

Within a few moments, we were airborne and headed to the Heavens.

After Maximus landed on the ground, we met up with Beacon and Nevaeh, both of whom ran up to us as soon as we got off the Winged Horse.

We both thanked them, and then we told the Archangel siblings that the Minotaur and Acanthus had both been defeated.

Chrysanthe showed them the vial of blood, plus the Utopian Sword, and then thanked Beacon for melding it together.

He smiled at Chrysanthe, before giving her a hug.

After backing away, he thanked her, and then Nevaeh spoke up.

All three of us: Beacon, Chrysanthe, and I, we all turned to look at her.

"Well then, if you have defeated both of the threats, then we can go see Hali. That way you both can be cured, as well as Viro and Thera, Chrysanthe."

I nodded and couldn't help but smile.

Everyone who had been affected could finally be cured.

And Chrysanthe had made that happen. Chrysanthe, once again, had saved everyone.

I smiled as I walked up to her, and she gave me a loving look as I wrapped my arms around her waist.

I picked her up and cradled her in my arms; she watched me for several moments before leaning forward and kissing my right cheek.

My face immediately felt warm from the contact.

I felt my thick, black wings protrude from my back, and then I was in the atmosphere in the span of a heartbeat.

Beacon and Nevaeh joined us as I landed right in front of the Heavenly Falls, where Hali would be visible in just a few moments.

I gently placed Chrysanthe on the ground, and she smiled at me once she was able to stand. My arms receded from her waist.

I looked at Nevaeh, who had a rock in her hand, and she glanced at Chrysanthe and I before throwing the stone so it would ripple in the Heavenly Water.

The movement created an interesting effect, and then the rock sank. I saw movement in the water, and then Hali came to the surface.

The water sprite looked from Nevaeh to Beacon to Chrysanthe to me, and smiled cordially at me before glancing back at Chrysanthe.

She rummaged through the pockets of her dress, and stopped when she found the vial of blood.

Hali swam up to Chrysanthe to get a better look, before taking the vial and inspecting it.

The Guardian of the Heavenly Falls grinned, and then opened the vial, so the bodily fluid could go into the Water.

She brought her eyes to Chrysanthe, before peering at the Utopian Sword, which was now, once again, clean and in Chrysanthe's chest, resembling a Fate Tattoo.

The sharp edge of the weapon poked out through the top of her dress.

Hali did a side glance over at me, moving her head a little bit.

Then she spoke.

"Well, Celio," Hali said before peering over at me, "and Chrysanthe," she looked over at my love, "you both have completed your task. You both have defeated the Hell Being known as Acanthus, and the Minotaur. Now that you both have collected the blood of the enemy and the blood of your own veins, you can save everyone that was affected by the Hellions. They can all be cured of their ailments."

She paused momentarily, before continuing.

Celio," she said, looking straight at me, "I am especially pleased by what you did after I gave you gills. Gills to help you retrieve the other half of the Utopian Sword. Now, you both can heal your wounds, along with anyone else who was affected."

I looked over at Chrysanthe, who walked to the Water, and then just submerged herself underneath the enchanted liquid.

The blood unlocked the Falls, so that Chrysanthe and I could jump in.

She surfaced and looked at her right arm, the one that had the map of our World, as well as the scar that wove in and out between the massive tattoo.

The scar from Thana, her evil fraternal twin.

When she turned to look down at her right arm though, the scar was gone.

It had healed.

I blinked in surprise, and then I saw Chrysanthe looking at me, before shifting her eyes to my shirt.

She peered up at my face, and then down to my shirt.

My face, and then my shirt.

I knew what she wanted, just from her body language.

She wanted me to come into the Water with her, so that I could heal the wound that Thana had given me.

Thana had stabbed me in the torso, and now I had a long scar.

One that could be healed with the liquid of the Heavenly Falls.

I took a deep breath, going over to the Water, and jumped in with all my clothing on.

When I surfaced, Chrysanthe was by my side.

I gulped in oxygen as I brought myself to the surface of the Water.

The air that entered my lungs tasted like Spring. The season where every plant was in bloom, causing a sweet scent to erupt throughout the Realm.

I inhaled deeply, filling my organs with the aroma. When I exhaled, I saw Chrysanthe swim toward me.

I smiled lightly when I saw her, and she watched my eyes as she brought her heavily tattooed right arm up out of the liquid so that I could look at it.

Chrysanthe kissed my lips lightly, and I grasped her right hand afterward.

Gently, running my fingertips along her skin, I saw her eyes flutter closed.

I gingerly touched her skin while inspecting her extremity, and saw the massive tattoo that was the map of our World.

But I didn't see the scar that had been magically woven in and out of the map.

I saw no scar.

"You're completely healed, Chrysanthe," I breathed. "You're healed."

Then, I paused.

The scar on my torso had stung slightly when I'd jumped into the Heavenly Falls.

But now, there was no pain.

My eyebrows furrowed, and I squinted as I automatically looked at my now drenched white shirt.

I brought my left hand up to my torso, feeling for the scar that was left by the Empyrean Blade when Thana had stabbed me.

I brought my fingers against my own skin, feeling for the puckered injury.

That was when a grin erupted over my face.

I couldn't feel the long scar anymore. I was healed.

Chrysanthe grinned before kissing me.

"Both of us are healed now, Celio," she said softly.

I heard the Water ripple slightly, and then turned to see Hali behind Chrysanthe and I.

"You both may bring the Healing Water to Viro and Thera. Here," she said, putting the vial that Chrysanthe had given her underwater.

Hali filled the vial with the enchanted liquid, before handing it back to Chrysanthe.

"Now, you can heal your parents, Chrysanthe," Hali said, to which Chrysanthe just smiled.

"Thank you, Hali. Thank you so much."

95

Chrysanthe

I grasped the vial of the Healing Water as I smiled at Hali, before I looked at Celio.

"Alright," I said, glancing at Hali, and then looking at my love. "Let's go heal Viro and Thera."

Hali smiled.

"Bye, Chrysanthe. Bye, Celio," the water sprite said, submerging herself under the enchanted water afterward.

I turned to Celio, my gaze breaking away from the Guardian of the Heavenly Falls, and he advanced toward me.

He picked me up and cradled my body in his arms.

I laughed as he gave me a quick kiss, and then his thick black wings appeared, and we both left the Afterworld.

Celio's arms wrapped around my frame as he hit the grass of the Earth.

My head was tilted into his chest so I could feel and hear his heartbeat.

My eyes opened to his soft voice, his breath fluttering onto my cheeks.

"Chrysanthe," he said, and my eyes opened to his face close to mine. "We're here."

I blinked away my slight drowsiness.

I smiled at my love, before bringing my right arm to his neck, shifting my body slightly so that my feet could land on the grass.

As always when Celio carried me, he waited until I was positioned upright and was stable before he took his hands away from my body, my waist.

I kissed Celio's cheek as soon as I had my balance, and a soft laugh shook through his throat.

I grinned at Celio, and then turned to see the cottage that had been made by Sybella for my parents.

I watched the cottage for a few moments, sighing before I began walking toward the small home.

Celio was not far behind me.

I inhaled deeply and exhaled slowly, the door to my parent's cottage right in front of me as I stood beside Celio.

I glanced at him for a split moment, and then knocked on the door.

"Mom?" I called. "Dad?"

I waited patiently, and then the entranceway opened, and my mother stood in front of me.

Her long, brown hair cascaded to her elbows, while her body was shaped like an hourglass.

Thera's eyes widened immediately. She was crying tears of joy as she engulfed me in a bear hug, a bear hug that was way too disproportionate to her size.

Mom buried her face into my shoulder, and then called for my father in a thick voice. "Viro! Viro, come here! Chrysanthe and Celio are here! Oh, honey, I missed you so much!"

Thera started to cry again, and I couldn't help it; I began to cry along with her.

I loved my parents so much...

"Chrysanthe, you're back!"

I heard a booming, intimidating voice, and Thera pulled away from me so I could see my father.

Viro.

Thera backed away from me, right as my father engulfed me in a bone-crushing hug.

"Chrysanthe," he said. "You saved us."

When both of my parents backed away, they turned their attention to Celio, who was still by my side.

Viro and Thera watched him for a moment before they both hugged my love.

I smiled as I saw my parents with Celio, and when they backed away from him, cordial grins were on their faces.

Viro and Thera glanced at Celio, and then at me.

The smile that was on my face grew wider as I saw how my parents appeared.

They appeared ecstatic to see Celio and I.

Especially after I gave Thera the vial that contained the Water from The Heavenly Falls.

The Water that could heal my mother and father, since she had been blinded, and he had been poisoned.

All from my twin, Thana...

The enchanted liquid would heal Viro and Thera and had already healed Celio and I.

Now, all four of us: Viro, Thera, Celio, and I, we all would be able to go to the Heavens. Go to the Heavens without burning up in the Everlasting Light that surrounded the Realm of the Archangels.

Thera's hands shook slightly as she held the vial with the Heavenly Water, but then Viro's hand went on hers.

"Here, Thera," he said. "Let me open that for you, my love."

I grinned.

My mother and my father were both still very much in love.

Viro opened up the bottle for Thera before he handed it back to her.

Thera drank half of the vial, and then gave it to Viro, who drank the rest.

Their body language changed within moments. Their backs straightened up, while the color came back in their faces. They blinked rapidly.

The effect of the Water was immediate; it seemed like it was only a few moments that Viro and Thera felt better. Rejuvenated and refreshed.

Both of them looked at Celio and I after drinking the liquid. Then they brought their eyes to my love.

"Now that we both have the Water from the Heavenly Falls in our system, would we be able to go back to the Afterworld now?" Viro asked Celio.

I could instantly tell that they wanted to go back immediately.

My parents were anxious to get back to the Heavens.

I glanced at them, and then brought my attention to Celio.

In my head, I was wondering the same thing.

Would they be able to go back? I thought.

But Celio just smiled, nodding understandingly at Viro's words.

"Yes, Viro. Yes, you both will be able to go back to the Afterworld." He paused for a moment or two, before asking, "Would you both like to go back to the Heavens now?"

They both nodded their heads simultaneously.

Celio smiled a light smile, and then turned to me, giving me a quick kiss before speaking into my lips.

"I'll see you once I get back, okay?"

He kissed me again, and I closed my eyes as I nodded.

"Alright, Celio," I said, looking into his hazel eyes before he walked over to both Viro and Thera.

He closed his eyes, said an incantation, and put both his hands on their backs.

Thick black wings erupted not only from Celio, but from Viro and Thera as well.

All three of them turned and looked at me, and then twisted back around, flying into the atmosphere, leaving me behind.

96

I burrowed down in the bedsheets as the wind gently brushed my skin, my cheeks.

I shivered slightly at the sensation, and almost, as if on cue, Caliya came and sat right beside my bed.

She blew air out of her nostrils as she moaned affectionately, and the tigress pushed her head into my chest.

I chuckled, petting her massive head and soft fur.

Smiling as I ran my hands over her ears and her muzzle, I just focused on Caliya, when I knew that he was back.

Celio was back from the Afterworld.

Even though he didn't make a sound, I could still sense him in the darkness of the night.

I smiled lightly as I sensed a change in the atmosphere, and I heard him speak through the blackness that was drenching our surroundings.

I blinked, before Celio spoke.

"May I join you?" he breathed.

The air from his lungs tickled my face, and finally I just rubbed my hands together, creating a ball of flame so I could see my love's features.

I put the fireball in a glass nearby, so that there was light in the room.

"There you are, Chrysanthe," Celio said gently, leaning forward and bringing his lips to my cheek.

A warm sensation rippled down my back when Celio pulled away to look in my eyes.

"May I? he asked.

"Yes," I responded in a whisper.

Celio approached the bed, climbing into the sheets.

He wrapped his arms around my body, kissing my forehead.

My eyelashes fluttered at the sensation, and then we fell asleep with our arms wrapped around each other.

97

The warm sensation of Celio's body heat was what caused me to open my eyes.

I was snuggled in the sheets with Celio's arms still wrapped around my body.

I smiled as I turned and saw his sleeping, calm face, and kissed his cheek as he breathed.

In and out. In and out. In and out.

He took in oxygen slowly, rhythmically, as his arms were wrapped around my waist, his palms on my abdomen.

I grinned as I felt his hand spread out over my belly, and a laugh went through my throat as I looked at my love.

I loved Celio so much...

I laid in the bed for a little while longer, watching his sleeping, calm expression, seeing his chest rise and fall as he breathed...

Caliya's orange, black-striped fur moved as I saw her stroll to the side of the bed, where I was.

She blinked her huge amber eyes as they focused on mine.

I smiled as I reached out to her with my left chrysanthemum-tattooed hand, and I rubbed Caliya's ears. The tigress let out a soft moan that shook through her entire body, including her muzzle.

A yawn made its way through my throat, and it was after that that I realized the sun was out. The illumination was streaming through my window.

"Alright, Caliya," I told the tiger. "Time to get up."

I turned to look at Celio's sleeping, content face, smiling and then kissing his cheek.

I gently took his hand off my abdomen, moving his arm slowly so I wouldn't startle him awake.

I carefully got out of the bed, and Caliya came to me instantly, throwing her massive head onto my abdomen as soon as she saw me hit the ground of the treehouse.

A soft, breathy chuckle went through my throat as I stroked Caliya's ears, causing a rumble to shake through her muzzle.

The sound rattled my skeleton with the amount of strength she had in her body, and I stroked Caliya's ears some more.

But when I brought my eyes to the treehouse window, I paused.

Black dust particles were in the atmosphere, swirling through the air.

I squinted, perplexed, and that was when I felt arms wrap around my body.

"What is that?" Celio asked, murmuring into my ear.

"I don't know," I said softly as I felt his palm on my abdomen once more.

The black dust came closer to the window, and I gulped as it blew through the air.

Whatever it was that was coming our way, it wasn't good.

It wasn't going to be good at all.

Glossary

Chrysanthe- (Chris-an-th)

Celio- (Seal-e-o)

Sybella- (Sigh-bell-a)

Beacon- (Bee-con)

Nevaeh- (Ne-vey-a)

Caliya- (Ka-lee-ya)

Cyra- (Sigh-ra)

Viro- (Vi-ro)

Thera- (Ther-a)

Hali- (Hal-ee)

About the Author

Elizabeth Wittekind has always had an active imagination and been creative. Growing up loving the fantasy genre in books and film, she began writing her debut, *Ethereal Imprints*, in 2017. She published the novel in 2022. *Ethereal Afterworld* is the sequel. Elizabeth has several additional works in progress.

Also by: Elizabeth Wittekind

Arcadian Divinity

The Ethereal Chronicles

Ethereal Imprints: Book 1

www.ingramcontent.com/pod-product-compliance
Lightning Source LLC
Chambersburg PA
CBHW020827260626
47169CB00003B/858